The Chaldean Prophecy

Yasmine Zahran

I0611576

Published by Nadir Khuri Publishing
ISBN 978-0-9982940-0-1
First Edition

.

This book is for dreamers, visionaries, antiquarians, adventurers and mystics as well as magicians and soothsayers.

*   *   *

The characters and events are fictitious but Syriacs, Chaldeans and Assyrians are real - so is Jerusalem! The monastery of Mar Murkus is also real but its occupants and events are imaginary.

Cover Design by Nadir Khuri M.D.
Cover represents Past, Present, and Future in the Chaldean Prophecy

Contents

Book I

Chapter I: Ill Met in Jerusalem

Chapter II: The God with the Two Faces

Chapter III: Encounter with Archangel Gabriel

Chapter IV: A Sufi in Mamluk Street

Chapter V: Genetic Makeup

Chapter VI: Espionage Oblige

Book II

Chapter VII: Introduction to the Report

Chapter VIII: The Report A: Evolution

Chapter IX: The Report B: Incarnation

Chapter X: The Report C: World Government

Chapter XI The Report. D: An Odiferous World

Chapter XII: The Report. E: Celestial Music

Epilogue

Tell those who claim knowledge of science, they
know one thing but many veiled remain.

Abu Nuwas (Abbasid poet, 8th Century)

Chapter I

Ill Met in Jerusalem

Could this have happened anywhere in God's universe, but in a narrow forsaken alley, reeking with rot, fried garlic, rancid oil of sesame and a subtle and repugnant odour of human decay with the rotten bones of generations buried in layer upon layer underneath the eroded pavement, Jerusalem,the holy, the austere, the necropolis, the home of cults, prophets, pseudo-mysteries and miracles. Jerusalem, the actress whose favourite role is playing the martyr, compelled to assume a new identity every few decades or centuries, for she is now being Judaized and she was once Romanized, Arabicized, Europeanized, but in all those roles she never shed her ancient and primary Canaanite roots.

I was treading, carelessly, its worn old stones on a misty Spring day on my way to visit a friend who lives in Khaski Sultan, on an intact Mamluk street near the Aqsa mosque, with crumbling palaces, domes and arches of the 14th century façades intact on the outside but broken into pieces and falling into dust on the inside a devastation that only time can achieve. I was looking forward to some happy hours inside one of these façades where I would read Sufi poetry with my friend and reminisce about old times when a certain bend on the road in the Christian quarter, brought back a long dormant flash of memory connected with this very spot suddenly hit my brain. I stood, mesmerized on the mark, where a long time ago my little hand was held tightly by my grandfather's rough and ulcerated one, pulling me away from the suffocating dense crowd as he cried "Hold tight little one, they are in a frenzy and they might crush us".

This was my first memory of the Medina –the city– for this is how they called Jerusalem in our village. The Medina was our city, the centre of our universe. Everything began and ended in Jerusalem. I was four years old and although I was told I was taken twice before to the Medina to the old Jewish doctor "Tichot", whose clinic in Sheikh Jarrah catered to Arab villagers, I have no recollection.

My grandfather, a tough and querulous old man acted as my surrogate father in the latter's absence, an absence that lasted from before my birth until I was 15 years old. But about this betrayal of a young beautiful wife and an unborn child I will not speak, for it is a pain I have not exorcised. It was natural for me not to have a father, only a long suffering mother whose anguish I wanted to carry, a burden for a child, but a mission accomplished for I did carry both our pains, a double legacy of chagrin.

6

The sudden flash of memory was perhaps due to the same weather condition and the same season, was in a day Jerusalem reverted to her Byzantine past, a past lurking in one of the layers embedded in the belly of Jerusalem that it never forgets.

It was the funeral of the aged Greek Orthodox Patriarch, a ritual which persisted after the fall of Byzantium, a fossilized clinging to the broken thread of history, for each of the five Patriarchs assumed part of the mantle of the fallen Emperor and clung to the archaic protocol of death, following in the footsteps of the Pope who, a thousand years earlier, assumed the role of the Roman Emperor of the West.

My grandfather, like all the clans of our village, was born as a Greek Orthodox, part of an ancient Arab Christian community which thrived under the Moslem Arabs from the Umayyad to the Ayyubid with an Arab religious hierarchy, until the coming of the Ottomans who put the Christian Arab community in matters of religion under the Greeks of Istanbul, a strange way of the conquerors appeasing the conquered by delivering to them the Christians of the Orient, a double slavery for the Christian Arabs, politically under the Turks and religiously under the Greeks, followed by the British who kept the status quo.

Nominally a Christian, my grandfather knew nothing about his religion except for the ceremonies of birth, marriage and death. The trip to the Medina for the funeral was an impulse due perhaps to an atavistic racial memory lurking in the darkness of his soul, a reversion to another age, for he was so excited by the procession and thrilled by the crowd in this very spot which clenched my memory many, many years after.

He raised me on his shoulders, straining his short thick neck and shouted above the din of the crowd "look, look, you will never see such a sight again". True, for after all these years I felt once more the thrill of seeing the *qawwas* , a remnant of the liveried guards in the service of patriarchs and foreign consuls in 19th century Palestine, and hearing the thuds of his silver staffs on the harsh pavement stones. He preceded the cortege of the mummified patriarch sitting regally on a throne carried by many hands above the heads of the crowd, the sparkling jewels of his tiara and the resplendent robes of yellow, red and green spun with golden thread, so brilliantly, that they reflected the sun in the dark alleys leading to the Holy Sepulcher. I clapped my hands as the procession drew nearer, which resulted in a rebuke from my grandfather in a harsh angry vive "you don't clap for the dead, child", but to me the Patriarch seemed alive with his pale skin and a shadow of a smile on his thin lips. "Sidi"[1], I said, "but he is not in a coffin, he cannot be dead".

The scene came back to me once before when I was poring over the history of Byzantine emperors in

---

1   Sidi – My Lord, the manner of addressing one's grandfather.

the university library, for I knew and the books did not, with what pomp emperors were sent to their graves.

The flash-back disappeared as suddenly as it came, as I tottered and wobbled in my high heels over the slippery pavement with a thrill the memory gave me. But above all I reveled in walking in the narrow passage ways between cluttered houses for I had desisted from coming to Jerusalem for some time because of the Israeli check points that littered the only road from my village to the city. At the beginning, I made a game of this inconvenience trying to outwit the Israeli patrol, but what really kept me away for a time was wallowing in the mud when changing taxis, a process that left me dehumanized, but finally neither checkpoints nor the high wall they built could keep me away from Jerusalem.

Deep in my reveries oscillating between the past and the present, my heart missed a beat as I felt a clammy hand on my left shoulder. I jerked my head back, full of fear, expecting one of the bands of the Russian mafia that held sway over prostitution and crime in the Holy City, or an audacious hungry beggar, but instead I was looking into the face of a withered, wizened man of an indefinite age, with the eyes of a serpent, in an oriental, priestly attire with a black rounded shining satin hat as a head dress and a staff of carved ivory and silver. I shrunk back speechless as the apparition said gently "Don't be afraid, Zuhra". I cut him short exploding with rage. "Who on earth are you, and how do you know my name? How dare you accost me in the street". I deliberately raised my voice to attract passers-by. "Please forgive this brusque way of attracting your attention. It is a long, long story. Please be indulgent and come with me to the Syriac monastery which is not far and there I will explain. I understand your reaction but I had no other way of contacting you". He hissed, and I again raised my voice. "There is still mail in this country and there are telephones". "We could not use those, we are under surveillance". "Ah", "I said "Is it for political intrigue that you catch me on the street?". The man gasped for breath and wiped his black bottomless eyes of a serpent with a dirty handkerchief. "I cannot explain in the street" he said in a pathetic voice. 'You will say what you have to say right here", I said angrily. "I have no time as I am on my way to visit a friend and will have to go back early to my village because of transport".

He started to shake his head from left to right and I was afraid he was on the verge of a fit. "What we need to say takes a little time. As to transport, to evade checkpoints we will send you back in a diplomatic car, which a friendly country puts at our disposal. Please come with me to the monastery of Mar Murkus[1], you have nothing to fear".

---

1   Mar Murkus – Saint Mark.

I hesitated. Maybe he is not a priest as he claims and this 'mise en scène' was orchestrated for robbery or kidnapping but then my addiction of haunting the monasteries and convents of Jerusalem took over, for strange as it was, I never visited the Syriac church and monastery. So with a reluctant curiosity I followed him as we turned back from the Christian Quarter until we came to Bab El-Khalil,(opposite the Citadel, between the Armenian and Jewish Quarters). There we turned right into the paved narrow, smelly alley of Mar Murkus where the Syriac church was located.

We stood at the patio between the miniscule church and the monastery, as he told me with pride that they were built on the site of the house of St. Mark the evagelist, and that it was the first and oldest church of Christianity. He then turned towards the monastery and said "Here in the upper room was the place where the Last Supper was held". I murmured "supposedly", but he turned a deaf ear to my doubt and continued "it is built on the site of the house to which the washing of the feet is ascribed at Pentecost" but when he saw the skepticism written largely on my face he said defiantly "Come now, I will show you the inscription of the 6th century AD, carved on the northern pillar inside the entrance of the church". His words were for me the "open sesame" as if he knew by instinct the magic that inscriptions held for me.

I followed him eagerly while he was fumbling to open the huge wooden door, with its two shining bronze crosses. I rushed inside to admire the little jewel of a church when I became aware of a woman in black who greeted me with a heavy guttural dialect of northern Iraq. I turned to the priest with a question on my face. "No, no she is not a Khaeta[1]. This is a monastery, not a convent". I could see he was eager to enlighten me so I asked him a question which launched an entire repertoire I was sure he recited to all visiting tourists.

This church has been destroyed and sacked by conquerors on a regular basis. It was first destroyed in 70 AD and repaired in 73 AD, destroyed again by the Persians during their conquest of Palestine and again by the Fatimid Caliph Al-Hakam in the 11th century (1009) AD. The period of the Crusades was nefarious for us and for our church, for the Fatimids exiled us by force to Egypt on the pretext that we might assist the Crusaders.   Meanwhile 700 Syriac Families from Edessa took refuge in Palestine when the Crusaders overran the country, but the church was massively destroyed. The amazing thing is that it was always repaired and rebuilt, after every destruction. He then pointed to me the parchment portrait of the Virgin Mary in its glass framework, believed to have been painted by St Luke with the Aramaic inscription underneath. "The Ottomans" he continued, "confirmed our right to this monastery in 1579 but this was

---

1   Khaeta – Nun in Syriac.

followed by massacres and persecution which led to our fleeing the monastery, leaving it empty for 276 years, until 1855 when it was repaired and reoccupied. You can see this inscription in Syriac over the door which gives the names and dates of all those who have repaired and rebuilt it".

When he stopped reciting his monotonous monologue I woke up to the fact that I still did not know why I was brought here and said to myself as I stood in the miniscule church "what irony this morning a flash of memory brought back Byzantine Jerusalem and here I stand in Mar Murkus church which evokes Aramaic/Syriac Jerusalem centuries and centuries before the Byzantines. Oh Jerusalem! what more tricks will you play on me, and what magic. But then I saw the bottomless eyes of a serpent staring at me and my fury mounted. "have you brought me here for a guided tour of the church? Why don't you tell me what this is all about?" The priest was crestfallen. "I wanted to give time for Abouna[1] the bishop, to prepare for your visit. We can go up now".

A huge iron door in the patio was opened with a screeching sound, which can only mean lack of use and yet there were monks living there. We climbed the stairs to the second floor where there was an open terrace with a profusion of geraniums in full bloom and

---

1   Abouna – Our father: the title by which Arabs and Syriacs call a priest.

13

tables and chairs, pleasantly welcoming, after the darkness of the church.

I took a seat for I was tired and troubled an aroma of incense filled the air, mixed with an odour I could not identify. The hag in black came with a tray of coffee and a plate of sweets. "The lady is a recent refugee from Mosul in Iraq" the priest said while she slurred the cacophony with a stream of words I could not follow. All I heard was a hard ka-ka-ka mark of the Mosul dialect. The priest interrupted her and said "This sweet is called the manna of heaven, the biblical manna, and is only made in Mosul. Try it, it is very good."

I shunned his sweets and said to him as I sat drinking the coffee 'you can talk now, I am all ears'. To my surprise he laughed. "You mistook me for Abouna the (Rabin) bishop, I am only the messenger". Why he found the fact amusing I did not know, but then I heard voices and shuffling of feet coming from the room opposite. "We will go now to the Rabin, please follow me".

I got up heavily from the chair for fear was taking hold of me. I felt that once I entered that room there would be no going back, no return to normality. The messenger priest must have sensed my fear for he tried to reassure me. "It is a great honour to be received by the holy man, he is so old and frail that the air around him is so rarefied that one does not dare to breathe in his presence". This was a semblance of a warning not to be brusque and tire the old man.

I entered a dark room with a musty decadent smell evidently out of use since Ottoman days. It had one window and two doors, an old sofa and three chairs with coffee tables as furniture. I was studying my surroundings when I heard the shuffling of feet at which the priest stood up to open the door for the apparition of a bent old man in a black soutane, supported on both sides by two acolytes. The priest bowed low and rushed to kiss his hand as I stood motionless. I knew that I should do the same, but I did not move and he did not stretch his hand but said in a voice that seemed to come from the beyond "Welcome, Ya Binti (my daughter) it is a happy hour that you are here'. He then refused to be helped and sat like a young man and with a gesture dismissed the priest and the acolytes.

I could not move in a sort of mental paralysis; I was only aware of the aroma that I thought must have affected my senses but then he spoke. "Sit down, my child. I know how you feel, and I ask you humbly to forgive this mise en scène. There was no other safe way to bring you here. We are under surveillance. Our letters are censored, our telephone is tapped and we had to accost you on the street. For your security, our connection must not be known. Your being here is a miracle, but life itself is a miracle out of the chaos and debris of the universe. And here I am despite my age and your youth and the generations and civilizations that divide us, calling on you to help me close a circle drawn more than a thousand years ago, to fulfill a vow and to pay a debt contracted to a dying man, so long, long ago.

He then stopped and said coyly as he wheezed out between bouts of coughing "admit you are curious to know my age, but I am acting like ladies who refuse to give their age – ha, ha, ha" and he suddenly stopped, realizing that I am still standing. "Won't you sit down my child?" "Abouna" I said harshly "with all the respect due to you I am shocked, puzzled and mystified. I want an explanation of why I am here". He hesitated before he said "Ah, ya binti, indulge an old man and allow him his little caprice. Before I explain your presence here I must give you the background, after which you will decide to accept or refuse this call. I shall speak to you freely, for I know that what I tell you will remain within the walls of this room. But I see a question on your face: how do I know I can trust you? It's because my child we have your psychological profile. You see, we have copied the methods of the Israeli Mossad, and particularly the American CIA. We have high officials of Syriac origin in that agency; our dispersal at times has advantages. You will find a Syriac, a Chaldean, and an Assyrian anywhere from India to Alaska. You are astonished for you did not think the Syriacs are that numerous or that modern? And he laughed, coughing and out of breath.

"You see we know your curiosity about the universe, your passion for history, your addiction to ruins and ancient manuscripts, but above all your pain and anguish for Palestine". I was in such rage my eyes were blurred and as I could not hit the old man as was my first reaction, I screamed interrupting him "Abouna, are you a bishop or an agent of the intelligence service? Who on earth gave you the authority to violate my private life? With what right did you probe my integrity, how dare you. This is moral rape. To whom do I complain? You took advantage that I am from a people under occupation with no government. Our laws are aborted. To what tribunal do I go to report this criminal act? I shouted myself hoarse and my tears of rage were flowing. I saw him rise from his chair, wobbling towards me, almost falling to the ground, saying incoherently, "I bow before your rage and indignation. I humbly ask your forgiveness" and he fell to the ground. With what power, I raised him to his feet I don't know. His eyes were those of a wounded animal and tears streamed down his face. "I know you will understand my child if you let me explain". "I am used to injustice" I said, "but this I cannot accept and I am not leaving this room until you explain to me why you intruded into my life, why?" I shouted.

He said nothing but rang the little bell on the side table and ordered coffee and was silent until the acolyte brought the coffee tray and closed the door.

"My child, I humbly beg your pardon again, for I was brusque and shocked you without meaning to. If you allow me, I have three long and different stages to explain in this affair. First, who I am and whom I represent, and second, the treasure above all treasures, the key to all this story, and third, your ancestors, the reason for your calling.

The mystery was getting deeper and in this unreal world the word "treasure" hit me, for it was again the "open sesame" of my childhood. It meant hordes of golden coins found by the villagers in ancient jars while ploughing the soil or golden jewelry in a tomb found by robbers. For our village was surrounded by ancient tombs and teeming with modern tomb robbers. I suppressed the thrill I felt and did not outwardly react, but when I looked at him he seemed disappointed, shrunken in his chair. I felt a pang of regret for he had humbled himself before me though my crudeness and intolerance were excessive. What if I listen to what he has to say, but I felt compelled to turn the subject around so I asked him in a voice in which I ironed out all resentment "Abouna, why have you called me at this moment in time? Why now?" My question pleased him for it set his mind on a different track and he was eager to respond. "Yes, why now my child, why not last year why not next year. The timing of this call has to do with death. Can you imagine that even with my very advanced age, death seemed to me far away and thus I kept putting off the encounter with you, as if I will live forever, until two weeks ago I felt a surge of vitality with the sap running through my veins. I was throbbing with life, my eyes cleared, you can see now the white of my eyes, instead of the yellow, my blotched skin cleared and I felt an exuberance, a joy in living which I had forgotten. I called for a mirror and could not believe the face I saw was mine. How could I explain it? It was a regeneration, my shriveled limbs and my leaden feet cried for movement. I came out of my retreat and for the first time in months shared life with the monks, drank wine and forsook my solitary frugal meals in my cell. I knelt in prayer to thank Allah for his benevolence and tried to find an explanation for this state of grace. I was overflowing with a sort of satisfaction – call it happiness – and I felt an urgent need to confide in someone. I decided to visit my only remaining friend and neighbor the Armenian patriarch who is very advanced in wisdom, although I normally dreaded the visit to the Armenian patriarchate for it is so large and boisterous while ours is so small and cozy. I walked the short distance between our two monasteries and he was struck by my changed appearance, as he exclaimed in his distorted Arabic. "Abouna my dear friend. You look ten years younger". "Your reverence", I said. "I came to seek an explanation for this phenomenon, this sudden surge of youth".

He ignored my question as we had coffee and small talk but he insisted I stay for lunch for he ordered my favourite dishes, Armenian pizza and pumpkin in tomato sauce and watched as I devoured the food with relish for the bitter dryness in my mouth had disappeared.

It was time for me to leave but he still did not answer my question so I said "Your reverence, your abstaining from giving me an explanation can only mean it is bad news". He scratched his forehead nervously before he said "I will not hide the truth from you, the state you are in is known in ancient mystic books and in long lost pagan religions, however, it survived in the oral tradition of many people, it is called 'wakefulness before death, an euphoric, ephemeral blossoming before the end of life, just like a candle that flares brilliantly before it is extinguished. Its duration varies in time from a few hours or days before death, to weeks and maybe months in some rare cases'. I cut him short for I saw how painful it was for him to speak of his imminent death. His eyes were moist and he started biting his nails. I lowered my eyes and took my leave.

He paused, short of breath and said "tut, tut, you induced me to talk about myself which is a bad sign of narcissism. I am grateful for this last glow at the end of my earthly days for it explains the urgency of my decision to meet you. My life has been full of joys and sorrows. I was an artist, a painter before I answered the

20

call of religion and I worshipped beauty as an attribute of God, and later I became an agent, not an intelligence agent as you surmised but an agent for the revival of my people, the Syriacs".

My people, who Arabs call the Siryan, are the true descendants of the Arameans, although with time they partly mixed with Assyrians and the Babylonians who are called the Chaldeans, for we speak the same language, Syriac, which is derived from ancient Aramaic. I need not tell you of the persecution and suppression my people suffered under different occupiers. We lost our land and our homes but we survived thanks to our language and our church. World War I drove us from our land in what is now southern Turkey which was really northern Syria. The new generation of Syriacs, Chaldeans and Assyrians after the calamity of the two World Wars began a movement for revival of our nation – a nation without land, alas, but for the preservation of our heritage and for this purpose, organizations sprang up where the Syriacs settled; some of them open and others secret. I interrupted "Abouna, you are a clergyman, where is the church in all this?"

The Church is the cornerstone of the movement. It is the church that preserved Syriac in its liturgy and gave us an identity. The Church is very involved in our national aspiration".

He paused, exhausted. I could not tell what he was leading to but in a way I was confused and flabbergasted. "Abouna, what have I to do with a Syriac revival?" I wondered if they, like the Jews, wanted a national home and said to myself Oh God, not in Palestine! What I asked was what all this had to do with me. I already have the burden of Arab nationalism badgered and attacked by enemies on all sides. The Syriacs may be persecuted, but we Palestinians are also a persecuted people striving for survival. I had had enough of emotion, shock and bewilderment and in reality I had learned nothing so far to explain my call.

I looked at Abouna who was trying to speak, but only groans and gurgles came out. His skin had turned greenish and he was gesturing feebly with this hands. I was struck numb. I rushed to him shouting "Abouna, Abouna" so that I could be heard, when the door opened and the messenger priest came in followed by the acolytes who carried him out of the room, but he was still gesturing towards me, trying to say something.

I walked out of the room, down the steps with blind rage, fie for his wakefulness he is going to die on me without an explanation. The messenger priest with his serpent eyes followed me to the patio. "Don't' be afraid, Zuhra, it is only a small crisis and it will pass. He was so well of late but the long séance was an emotional strain. I dismissed the priest saying, I will

22

find my way. He handed me copies of articles saying "Abouna wanted to give you these".

I walked up the alley blindly towards Bab El-Khalil. I was in no state to visit my friend on Mamluk Street, a name I gave to the street instead of "Khaski Sultan". I walked down to the Christian quarter where the priest had accosted me earlier, looking with vacant eyes at the souvenir shops while the shopkeepers bored without tourists were trying to entice me with their amber beads, pleading with me to buy candles and fake icons and cheap souvenirs made in China and Taiwan, but underneath and beyond their clipped Jerusalem dialect I heard the ancient sounds of bygone days, gibberish Genoese, guttural Turkish and the Arabic dialect as spoken in the time of Salah Ed-din, my head was turning and my dazed look made a shopkeeper invite me to sit inside and to offer me a cup of tea.

I am vague about how I arrived home and how many check points I passed or how many taxis I took in between.

The day that began with Byzantine recollections ended with the heavy Aramean strata, of which I was completely ignorant. Ironic that I left the monastery of Mar Marcus, as I entered it, ignorant of what it was all about with only gibberish talk about a national revival and a treasure. My fury rose as I reviewed my day in the city, perfidious Jerusalem, leading me on in the

23

alleys of its past, treacherous Jerusalem, changing faith and masters as regularly as the orbit of a star.

Chapter II

The God of the Two faces

Bewitched and abused I went back to my village with my resentment rising to a crescendo at the words of Abouna for I could not make out the three things he spoke of: the Syriac national movement, a treasure, a payment of a debt to a dead man and my ancestors, but what have they to do with each other or with me! My curiosity about the Arameans and their descendants, the Syriacs, was mixed with a culpability due to my semi ignorance of an ancient civilization that was the background of Arab civilization, so I ransacked my small library to find only general bits and pieces, but then I turned to the brochures and documents the messenger priest with the serpent's eyes had given me. The brochures were about persecution and massacres of the Syriacs by the Turks and Kurds in southern Turkey. What struck me was that the world knew about Armenian massacres but ignored the massacres and the exodus of Syriacs who inhabited southern Turkey which was in reality north Syria. It was the exodus and dispersal of a whole population which took refuge where it could, but this was modern history after the first world war. I had to delve back to much

26

more ancient days. To think that Syria which is now divided into four states, Syria, Lebanon, Jordan and Palestine (Israel, the West Bank and Gaza) was once known as Aram and ruled by Arameans for a thousand years. Their language, Aramaic was spoken by the then civilized world, the whole Orient and Persia, and was spoken by Christ which lead some Aramean enthusiasts to claim Jesus as Aramean. The fact that Jesus spoke and preached in Aramaic gave birth to many legends, one of which claimed that Jesus was not mentioned in the gospels between the age of thirteen when he appeared in the temple and thirty when he started to teach because he had spent that time in the land between the two rivers, where he studied religions and philosophy under the Chaldeans before he returned to Palestine. Dialects of Aramaic were spoken by Palmyran and Nabatean Arabs, who gave the alphabet to Arabic, the language of the Holy Qur'an.

The Arameans mixed and assimilated with their predecessors, the Canaanite/Phoenicians in Syria on the Mediterranean, and dwellers of Assyria of Babylon and established their kingdoms between Syria and Iraq, namely "Aram Naharin" (between the two rivers' and "Aram Badan" (Aram of the fields), and the Kingdom of Damascus. They were contemporaries and sometimes enemies of the kingdom of Israel in north Palestine and they stood for more than a century in the face of Assur, the greatest military kingdom the ancient world has ever known. In their struggle against

27

Assur they formed a coalition of twelve neighbouring kingdoms. Their king 'Adad Azar" succeeded in unifying all Syria, and had at his disposal the navy and the vast wealth of Phoenicia. Before leading the coalition to battle he prayed to the chief God of Aram, Adad, who was Baal to the Cannanite/Phoenicians saying "I shall fight for the land you gave us Great God, the land of fruit, wheat and barley. Tomorrow I will lead the army to fight your enemies the Assyrians. Tomorrow I will go through fire to enable your subjects the Arameans to plough their fields and plant their vines. Tomorrow the fate of Syria will be decided!

The fate of Syria was decided in 854 BC by the defeat of the Aramean coalition by Schalmanasser III who boasted in an inscription: "I, Schalmanasser III, king of Assur in the 18th year of my reign, crossed the Euphrates for the sixteenth time. Adad ben Azar king of Aram depended on this army, but I defeated him and accepted the submission of the kings of Tyre and Sidon. I departed from Ninevah and crossed the Tigris. I crossed the Euphrates on rafts made of goat skins. When I approached Aleppo, the inhabitants were seized by feet in subjucation. I received silver and gold and offered sacrifices to 'Adad', god of Aleppo. I destroyed, tore down and burned his (the Aramean king's) royal residence. He brought along to help him 1,200 chariots, 1,200 cavalrymen, 20,000 foot soldiers. King Ahab of Israel brought 500 soldiers, Jindub of

Arabia 1,000 camels, twelve kings were against me they faced me for a decisive battle. I fought them with the mighty forces of Assur. I inflicted a defeat upon them between the towns of Karkara and Gilza[1].

Aram, however, regained its strength after this colossal defeat and continued its struggle against Assur. One of their kings Haza-el repulsed the attacks of Shelmanasser twice and conquered the kingdoms of Israel and Judah, because the chief god of Aram Adad ordered him to destroy Israel and to enslave its armies so they would till the land of Aram. The king of Israel Juno Ahaz pleaded with the Aramean king in the name of his god Jehovah and in the name of Adad to allow him a thousand knights and a thousand chariots but Haza-el answered that Israel and its population were the slaves of Aram, but he allowed Juno-Ahaz 50 knights and 10 chariots so he will remember forever their slavery to Aram. The struggle between Aram and Assur went on for a hundred years after the destruction of the capital Karkara until Taghlath Pilazzar, the third (744-727 BC) decided on breaking the power of Aram forever. The last bastion of Aram was Damascus and the king Razin asked his people to shelter within the walls of the city, but thousands of refugees from the countryside were ravaged by famine and disease which distressed the king so that he cried in agony:

---

1   James Pritchard, Editor, the ancient Near East, vol. 1. Trans. A Leo Oppenheim, Princeton University Press, 1958, pp. 189-190.

Give me ashes to cover my head, destroy my golden and ivory throne, spill the flacons of precious ointments and perfumes – Oh Damascus! What has the enemy done to you and what is the fate of your luscious gardens".

Damascus was destroyed and the Assyrian Taghlath Pilazzar boasted: "like a rat Razin, the king of Damascus hid within his walls like a bird in a cage, he closed the doors but I entered Damascus; I killed its king; I burned its gardens; I cut the trees, the pride of the city. Not one of its inhabitants did I allow to flee. Those who survived I exiled beyond its walls". With the fall of Damascus in 732 BC, the political hegemony of Aram was over but the Arameans did not disappear from the stage. They monopolized the trade of interior Syria, as the Canaanite/Phoenicians monopolized that of the sea coast. Their cultural role came with the spread of their language which travelled along the trade routes and became the language of culture and commerce and the official language of governments in the fertile crescent. It replaced both the Hebrew and the Canaanite languages but it was not confined to the fertile crescent, for in the 5th century BC, under Darius, it became the official language of the Persian empire and remained so until Alexander the Great. It was a strange case of victory for a language that was not supported by a political power. They took the Phoenician alphabet and spread it to Asia. The north Arabs took the alphabet from the

Nabateans. The language was split into the eastern dialect from which grew the modern Syriac and the western which was the language of the Arab Palmyrans and Nabateans.

With the coming of Christianity the Arameans called themselves Syriacs to distance themselves as Christians from the pagan Arameans and gradually merged with the population, Cannanite/Phoenician in Syria and Assyrian Babylonian in Iraq while the Babylonians called themselves Chaldeans and not to be outdone by the Arameans who claimed Jesus, they considered Abraham the progenitor of Judaism, Christianity and Islam, a Chaldean, as his native land was Ur of the Chaldeans.

With this historical background I tried to place my call to the monastery in the right context, hoping that I would understand what the mystery was all about. However, one thing was clear, the ancient enemies, Arameans, Assyrians and Babylonians (Chaldeans) are grouping together because of their historical and linguistic links, aspiring for a national revival to preserve their heritage and their language and to regain their human rights.

When the call came I was genuinely glad to see Abouna enter the little room seemingly in better health and good spirits but I had to wait for the coffee and the Iraqi sweets called "Kletche" before Abouna apologized for having had his 'crise' as he called it. "I cannot die now, my dear child, before I fulfill my promise and yet I have qualms and misgivings for laying this heavy burden upon you. But now tell me what you thought of our last meeting?" "Abouna" I said 'I have been consulting history books but I want to know from you about the Aramean descendants, the Syriacs or as we Arabs call them 'Siryan'. "Tut, tut", he chuckled, "I expected you would. The Syriacs are sometimes called the Jacobites and are Orthodox, but differ from the Greek or Russian Orthodox in that they are "Monophysites", who believe in one nature of Christ, both human and divine, while the Greek Orthodox believe in a double nature, one human and one divine. We speak the same language as the Babylonians of Southern Iraq (who are known as Chaldeans and who were Nestorians until converted by the popes to Catholicism in the 16th century) and the Assyrians of north Iraq. We all had our share of Persian and Roman persecution but we in Syria were protected by the Ghassanids and yet we had to wait till the Arab conquest and Islam to freely practice our religion, but all this you know".

I then asked Abouna whether it is true that the Arameans claim Jesus, because he spoke their language, considering that it was the language spoken in Palestine during that period. "Ah, that", he said "It is a very old tradition but not only because he spoke the language, you remember that he was from Galilee which was not part of any Jewish kingdom, until the

32

Macabees conquered it and judaized it by force only one hundred years before Christ was born. The natives of Galilee were not Jews, but Syriacs converted to Judaism by force". "No, no" I interrupted. "You forgot that Galilee was conquered by the Macabees from the Itureans, an Arab tribe which ruled parts of Lebanon and Jordan beside Galilee and that the judaized natives were Arabs". "Tut, tut" Abouna said, piqued. "The base of the population was Syriac but my child to the world Jesus was a Jew and who is going to listen to you and me saying he is Syriac or Arab" "Abouna" I said wearily, historians know that Galilee was forced into Judaism, conquered from the Iturean Arabs, they also know that Herod, king of the Jews, who built the temple, was an Arab from the kingdom of Edom in southern Palestine, also Judaized by the Maccabees by force and yet to the world he is known as a Jew.

I then asked him about the ancient Aramean religion. Abouna was amazed and taken aback. "you realize my child that you are asking a Christian bishop about pagan gods?'" and he laughed and winked at me. "True", he continued "our ancient religion is part of our heritage, the chief god Hadad, Adad or Hudu another name for Baal, is the ruler of the clouds and the god of lightning and thunder. He was a two-faced god, a god of mercy and a god of fear and vengeance. Our invocations to Adad were imitated by the Hebrew psalms but wait, you can judge for yourself' Abouna rang the bell and the messenger priest who was always lurking behind the door, appeared and bowed. 'Please ask the young Mulki to come".

A young slim adolescent appeared, kissed the hand of Abouna and stood with his head bent until he was asked to recite the psalms of Adad. The youth closed his eyes, bent his head and recited in a melodious voice.

> *"The voice of Hudded on the water*
> *The god of glory thunders*
> *The voice of Hudded on high*
> *The voice of Hudded in like cymbals*
> *O, Lord of mercy*
> *The land of Aram has gone dry*
> *Command the storms to rise*
> *Command the rains to fall*
> *Have mercy*
> *When you appear before your people in the wilderness*
> *The earth trembles*
> *Command the heavens to rain*
> *Kadish, Kadish, Kadish (Holy)*
> *May Hudded's name be glorified".*

All was silent. I was struck dumb by the beauty of the hymn. "This is incredible" I said "It is like the Hebrew psalms". "Did you read the Canaanite psalms of Ugarit, Prayers to the Semitic gods resemble each other and who knows who copied who, but wait, you must hear invocations to his other face, the god of vengeance and fear" and he made a sign for the young acolyte who recited:

"Avert your anger from your people, Ho Hudded

Hudded the god of fear

Hudded the god of anger

Hudded the god of revenge

The monk suddenly stopped, by a gesture from the hand of Abouna who asked me 'Did you hear enough?" "Yes", I said, "this God frightens me; I remember now that he holds a hatchet in his hand and I neither like his thunder nor his lightning, but I would like to know about other Aramean gods".

Abouna seemed pleased as he said, laughing, "It seems to me that the Arameans were more feminists than most of their contemporaries, for the goddess Ashtar, wife of Hudded, eclipsed her husband, for her worship continued long after his, until the second century AD. She had more temples and priests.

Escalon was the center of her worship in Palestine which extended to Greece and Italy where she was assimilated with the Greek Aphrodite and the Roman Venus. You may be amazed by the domestic scenes between the spouses, for Hudded was furious when she went, with her head uncovered around the markets of Aram. She defied him as he had no power over her for she was the goddess of life and fertility, but he kept reminding her of her status as his wife and as such no wife in Aram goes out with her head uncovered or unveiled, and he went so far as to threaten her, with thunder and storms and of preventing the rain to fall, till the earth turned dry but if she persisted he would turn his face away from her".

I interrupted him. "What! Arameans know the veil!" "Yes", he said, "so did the Assyrians. The law decreed head dress for the wives and daughters of free men". "What other gods did they have?" I asked. "Shamsh, sun worship was known by all the Semites. There was also Rukab and Sahar, the god of the moon". I was lost in wonder and then I said aloud "To think that after a thousand years of rule the only thing left of the Syriacs today is the church with its Syriac liturgy". "Ah, you must look behind appearances, search for them in the blood of the people of Syria and in the names of months and in place names. There is hardly a village in geographical Syria which does not have an Aramaic name".

He was silent so was I for I suddenly was transferred back from one world to another. I felt bewildered. Was I in a Christian convent or in an Aramaic sanctuary where the young monk recites Psalms to Hudded and where Abouna, the bishop incarnates the role of the chief priest of Hudded. The monastery has many layers behind its shining façade and a vague recurrent apprehension ran over me until I shuddered "what was the game being played"? O Jerusalem, I murmured, only in your belly, in your hidden recesses such games can be played. How many cults, how many hidden mysteries are in you alleys?

At this point I automatically rose from my chair. "Abouna", I said 'I did not come here for a lesson in history". A statement I immediately regretted for it was I who provoked the return to the past. I then said humbly "So far I am still in the dark".

"You put me to shame, my child. I pray for your indulgence and your patience. I can only explain one thing at a time. Who am I, you ask, the Syriac bishop of Jerusalem or the chief priest of Hudded. Come, come do not protest. I know what you were thinking half an hour ago" and he smiled as I sat down, flushed, squirming in my chair at his uncanny reading of my thoughts. "But, Abouna..." I tried to put in a word "I am both my child. Hudded, the Psalms and his rebellious wife are part of our history, and our heritage, which we hope to preserve, revive and resurrect. You, yourself described us as fossils – rejects of history, but the fact that you are facing an old Syriac fossil is proof that there is still some life left' and he laughed grotesquely at his own joke. "We are aiming, my child, at no less than a renaissance of our civilization". Here, I interrupted "Who are we?" After a pause he repeated 'We are a nation without a home. We have taken refuge all over the world. Our ancient cities of Edessa (Urfa), Mardin, Amida (Diyar Bakr) seats of Syriac learning are now inhabited by Turks and Kurds. Most of our villages in north Iraq are now inhabited by Kurds. We are scattered throughout America, Europe, India, Syria and Iraq. Our last revolt against the Byzantines was in 708 in Antioch, which was crushed by the Emperor Phocas and his General Bonosus. The Ghassanids who protected us were by then broken and diminished but in their heyday in the 6th century they gave us our identity in a separate Monophysite church with a liturgy in Syriac instead of Greek. It is this church that saved us from extinction. It was the great Ghassnid king, Harith bin Jabla. Who, with the help of the empress Theodora nominated Jacob Bradeaus as bishop, and so the church was set up". He stopped breathless, his eyes sparkling like a youth".

A bell rang through my brain when he mentioned the "Ghassanids". Could it be that I was called because they assumed I was a Ghassanid descendant? If so, not only they are fools, but imbeciles, for this descent is only a claim by my tribe based on an ancient oral tradition and there is no tangible historical proof, but

38

Abouna intruded on this line of thought by saying 'I must go on with my tale. There is a new movement, my child, which insists that Syriacs, Chaldeans and Assyrians are one people with a shared history and language and therefore they must merge together as a political necessity. But patience, my child, I will come to the point which may answer one of your many questions. I talked of a treasure of which we hold a part in this monastery, the other half is now lost and must be found. The treasure is claimed by three groups as their heritage and was a reason for contention. However things have changed. Here is a high committee of nine members, three members from each group, which acts as a surrogate government, oversees all the problems and plans for the future. This committee, on my insistence had taken up the question of the treasure under its wing and asked me as the bishop who holds half the treasure in Jerusalem to take the responsibility of finding the lost half and had put in my hands the means to do so. Here he paused breathless. "I accepted the offer but on condition that I hand the recuperated treasure to its rightful owner, the owner designated by the bishop who whisked the treasure out of Hira on his death bed.

I was shocked. "Abouna" I said 'You enlightened me on many points, but I am still in the dark. What is this great treasure that you keep as a mystery and what is my role in all this? What have I, a Palestinian girl, who has enough of the Palestinian problem to do with a Syriac renaissance? Do I have Syriac blood? I assure you that this is a false route. I know you are playing for time to see perhaps if you can trust me. I do not say this to offend you, but what are you trying to recruit me for?" "Tut, tut, my daughter, I am humbled by your perspicacity. I am not taking time to see if I can trust you, but I am feeding you bits of information so that you can digest the whole when it is revealed to you and with your permission I would like to tell you how half the treasure was brought to Palestine. But let us have some coffee and some sweets" and he rang the bell to give his order to an acolyte.

I was befuddled. My mind was racing with bald guesses what could this treasure be? A horde of ancient gold coins, precious stones, a relic of a saint, a holy icon, or a piece of the cross or a sacred book. But where do I come in? The idea of recruiting me for their national movement was absurd. I was so absorbed in my thoughts that I jumped out of my chair when I heard a gurgle from Abouna's throat. I looked at him and there were all the signs of the last crisis, Ya Allah, I said over and over again. It is a very convenient crisis when Abouna wants to stop the narrative. I called for help and left the room before they carried him out. I refused to hear the explanation of the messenger priest and with what relief did I run down the steps to the patio and the narrow alley to escape the heavy atmosphere of the monastery, with that aroma of incense which I normally enjoyed but which began to oppress me. I ran raggle taggle, bumping into passers-by all the way to Bab-Al-Khalil, where the black sedan was waiting.

Back home I reflected coldly and calmly about the situation I was thrown into against my will. I toyed with the idea of not going back to the monastery for I felt abused, fallen into the hands of maniacs. Abouna was playing cat and mouse with me and who knows if the attacks of Abouna were not simulated?

The whole thing smelled of intrigue, but I was torn between curiosity and indignation. What enticed me was the treasure, but did the treasure really exist or is it all a trap set to snare me? But before making a decision I set to read all the articles and brochures that I was given published by various groups of Chaldeans in Detroit, Syriacs in Sweden and others. Most of these articles were in both Syriac and Arabic for most of these groups were Arabic speaking. The articles indicated a real desire for national revival and preservation of an ancient heritage with which I fully sympathized. I oscillated between refusal to go when the call came, but the obsessive desire for the secret of the treasure took over.

Abouna I was sure, will know in his uncanny way of my unspoken resolve, but then I realized that despite all the pitfalls, all the veils of mystery I sympathized with Abouna, with his frailty and his sad, wounded eyes and I decided to go to the monastery for the last time.

Chapter III
Encounter with the
Archangel Gabriel

Back in the monastery Abouna received me with a rare smile but he was only a shadow of his former self, a skeleton, skin and bones. "You see, my child, the awakening before death is wearing off and I return to my former state. More reason for me to speed this process, but let us have our coffee and manna of heaven first before we talk about the man who is at the root of this tale". True to my resolve I wanted to tell him that I wanted to pull out if he did not clarify the matter but I saw his hands trembling, unable to hold the coffee cup which he put down without drinking, and I did not have the heart to recite my ultimatum but to my surprise, he read my thoughts in his uncanny way and in a hardly audible voice he started "It all began in Iraq (Mesopotamia) where an Arab tribe, the Banu Lakhm founded a kingdom with a large army and developed a naval power which attacked the coastal cities of Persia in 325 the Persians invaded the Lakhmids, captured their capital Hira and massacred the population. The Persians made of Hira a buffer zone between them and the Byzantine. The Lakhmids became thereafter the rivals of the Ghassanids. Hira was the birth place of the Arabic alphabet. The Lakhmids remained pagans because the Persians frowned at the idea of their adopting Christianity, the religion of their Byzantine enemies, only their last king was Christianized but the Lakhmids refused Zoroastrianism, the religion of their masters. Hira became a centre for the Nestorian sect with a large Christian Arab community called (Ibad), however a minority followed the Monophysite creed and installed a bishopric in Hira between the 6th and 7th centuries.

The Monophysite bishop of Hira, known as a holy man was a primary target of Persian persecution so he went into temporary hiding until he could arrange a flight to Roman territory across the desert where the Monophysites were protected by the Ghassanid king. The bishop knew that he risked his life whether he stayed or fled but calculated that the risk was less if he fled, with something that he could barter for his life if caught by the Nestorians or the Sassanid. The only thing that he could think of was the Chaldean treasure which was kept heavily guarded in a monastery on the outskirts of Hira, built on the site of an ancient Chaldean pagan sanctuary. At this point of the narrative I jumped from my chair 'Abouna, what was the treasure?" for treasure hunts were the excitement of my childhood, but Abouna raised his hand to silence me 'all in good time, my child" and heedless of my questions he continued the narrative.

The idea of laying his hands on the treasure obsessed him and in the process the holy man became a thief. The bishop was helped in this scheme by many in the Ibad community who made it possible for him to whisk the treasure away so that he could buy his life. The bishop never disclosed the methods used for the theft nor how many of those who helped him were caught, tortured and executed after his flight, but the rumour circled that he was helped by a blind man who retired from the service of the monastery housing the treasure, and receiving as a reward for his service a large amount of gold. Whether the bishop was penitent for this heinous crime we do not know but the monk, a member of this monastery who tended him in his last illness, said that he spoke incoherently of the "treasure drenched with blood". Luckily we have details of his flight and his journey from Hira to Sergiopolis through an account he wrote before his death and which Behnam our monk brought back to Jerusalem. The account is written in Syriac but we have an Arabic translation made upon the demand of an eleventh century Rabin of this monastery". Abouna rang the bell and an acolyte appeared. He gave him instructions in Syriac, which was unusual for they all spoke Arabic in my presence. We were both silent until the acolyte came back with a box which smelled of rotten hide and from which he pulled a manuscript, handed it to

Abouna and withdrew. Abouna gazed at the sheaths of paper with unseeing eyes "Alas my sight is so weak I can hardly read but here is the account of the journey of the bishop" he said as he handed me the manuscript.

My eyes fell immediately upon the name of the translator, a certain Borsom from Edessa. I read aloud as Abouna added "Borsom came as a refugee to this monastery just before the arrival of the crusaders to Jerusalem and before the Fatimids moved the Syriacs of Jerusalem to Egypt. If you look at the bottom of the page you will find the name of the bishop who requested the translation". I tried to interrupt him but before I opened my mouth he anticipated me-by saying "All in time, all in time" and then "forgive me for not spending more time with you today but I feel very tired and I beg to retire", Being dismissed so abruptly I took my leave and ran all the way to the waiting car. Back home, I could not wait to read the account of the journey for it is not given to me every day to have a genuine 6th century document in my hands.

On the second page was the name of the author, the most reverend bishop of Hira and the title "A record of my journey from Hira to Sergiopolis, written on my sick bed, in the hostel of the apostles, near the tomb of the blessed Saint Sergius".

The following pages were supplications and laments. " I cry with Christ, why hast thou abandoned me?" "Alluhu, I sinned to save my body and lost my soul". "Woe unto the Persians, may the fire they worship be extinguished forever". "Give me ashes to pour on my head". This last cry seemed familiar for it was the cry of the ancient Aramean king of Damascus when besieged by the Syriacs. "Woe unto the man abandoned by his Creator. I am ravaged with fever and haunted by Nestorian sleuths who clamour for my death". "The following lines", wrote the translator, "were blurred and erased by water, probably tears".

After the confused lamentation came a well written text:

'I, Ephrem, bishop of Hira, beloved of the Ibad, fell under Persian wrath and in fear I sinned in the eyes of the Lord. In atonement for my deed I write an account of my flight and journey so that whoever reads it in the future will wonder at the just and balanced ways of Alluhu., for he inflicts a penalty for evil. I, who suffer the penalty am in the 37th day of my malady lying on a bed of straw in the hostel of the apostles in Sergiopolis. I arrived in this city already stricken with fever on a night without stars, which led some kind fellow travelers to bring me to this hostel where, heedless of my state, I threw my belongings and set immediately to seek the Ghassanid king, who I was told was on his yearly pilgrimage to the shrine of St Sergius. I tread warily on an unknown road, where I could hardly keep my balance for I had acute pain in my right ear. I accosted the few pedestrians on the road 'Where is the king's palace?" I asked, until I arrived at a high gate, with Arabian soldiers standing guard. "Halt! Where are you going ya sheikh? They asked kindly as I pushed my way forward. "I came all the way to see the king" I said wearily. "Steady old man" as they held my arms "why are you seeking our king?" "I want to hand him a treasure, person to person". The guards laughed at the idea of a beggar like me, for I was dressed as one, handing a treasure to the king they certainly thought I was demented. I was furious and shouted "Your king's tent and palace are open to all seekers, including beggars like me! He does not repulse anyone from his door. Why are you holding me from the king?" Tears of rage were rolling down my cheeks. "Alas, ya old sheikh, our king is gone, Harith bin Jabla left Yesterday to join his army at the frontier post on the Red Sea, Where the Persians are massing for attack" "What! The king is gone? I missed the king". I fell to the ground at their feet. They raised me and gave me water to drink. "We will give your treasure to the king" they said, humouring a mad old man. "No, no I shouted. I will give him the treasure with my own hands. I will follow him to the end of the earth". The guards shook their heads with pity for my foolhardiness and said "To follow our king you have to go from battlefield to battlefield from one frontier port to another. You cannot possibly follow his trail but you seem a stranger in this town. We will take you to the Madafa where you can dine and sleep". I thanked them, telling them I had already tasted Ghassanid hospitality but that I left my things in the lodging.

I steadied myself and walked back to the hostel, muttering loudly to anybody who could hear. "Tell me my friends, where oh where has the king gone?"

I arrived at the hostel, half dead, and threw myself on the straw bed without supper and without sleep. Oh how long the night is long: how could I wait until dawn? So, on the spur of the moment I decided to mitigate my vigil and my pain by writing, putting down the record of my journey from Hira to Edessa to Sergiopolis, lest I forget for I am afraid of the lapse of memory. On events before the journey I shall draw the veil, for if the facts seep out, my few remaining friends in Hira will pay the price. True, I committed a spiteful act, under the illusion that I had a right to the treasure, for am I not a Chaldean?

I fled Hira one night with two faithful acolytes who insisted on sharing my Calvary despite my protests for they were pampered youths used to comfort and easy life and who could not envisage the hardships ahead, for we could not follow the regular routes trailed by caravans and had to take untrodden pathways in case we were pursued after the discovery of the loss.

I prepared for the journey across the desert with the names of wells and oasis on the way and a map of Roman forts on the frontier with Persia. We had two camels loaded with food, medicine and water.

Soon enough the youths showed signs of fatigue and boredom and started each day with endless complaints. The first tragedy struck when one of the pack animals stumbled, injuring its feet and could not move. We had to leave the poor animal to die in the heat for we had no heart to kill it for meat, and had to carry on our backs some of its load and threw out the rest. Soon enough the youths began to sicken which made our pace very slow. I had to ration the food and water and was obliged to have them rest at intervals which exposed us to danger for pursuers were on our track.

I begged them to go back and say that I forced them to flee with me but they refused. We roamed the desert blindly hoping to arrive by miracle at the Euphrates, but then the second camel fell dead. My dilemma was to carry a heavy load on my back and to nurse the two sick youths who kept asking me to leave them to die. One morning I awoke after a troubled slumber at the feeble cries of one of the youths for his comrade had died during the night out of exhaustion. We had no strength to bury him so we left him lying in the wilderness, exposed to the elements, with tears streaming down our parched skin.

The only provisions left were a few dates and dry biscuits with a little water that tasted bitter. I abstained from drinking water to give it to the sick youth who, like his friend, gave up the ghost in a dreary night, where for once the desert seemed to darken without stars. I was too weak to cry for the two dead youths with their lives cut unachieved, because of me and in self-pity, alone in the wasteland. I threw the rest of our belongings and waited longing for death, but I felt such pity to leave the treasure that I robbed carrying it next to my skin in the desert amidst sands and stars. The more I wished for death the more I clung to the treasure and the gold coins, I had sewn in my tunic and my belt. I was delirious and kept repeating "I must cross the Euphrates and reach Roman territory where I will be safe". The few drops of water could not quench my thirst and I walked and walked in the blazing sun having no idea of the distance covered. I was half blind from the haze, but lo, what joy. I could not believe my eyes for I glimpsed palm trees in the distance with black Arab tents. I knelt to thank Alluhu, and dragged my leaden feet towards the oasis. Could paradise be other than an oasis of green and water? Alas, alas, the longer I walked, the more the oasis vanished as a mirage and before me stretched a horizon of nothing but burning sand.

I walked I stumbled and dragged my feet. For how long I did not recall. I only prayed for death, pleaded for death and for the treasure on my back I cared no more.

In deep despair I lay, on the burning sand when I saw out of the corner of my eye under my veil, an Arab on a camel coming towards me. And behind him there seemed to be a caravan with loaded camels. I was overjoyed. I raised myself up saying, I would live, ah for some water, and suddenly before me there was only a void, no Arab, no camel, no water, only wind and sand and more sand. I screamed, but my voice was dim. "Alluhu is merciful, but nature is cruel. Why give hope to a dying man who is left in the starkness of the heat with nothingness. Would I not give my soul for a nebulous sky".

I dragged myself slowly, dreaming of water until my legs would obey me no longer. I curled myself up as If I were in the womb and entrusted my soul to Alluhu's keeping, for my eyes were sore, my lips parched and my tongue dry like a stone and I must have drifted off into the world of sleep from which there was no waking. I did not know for how long I lost consciousness for when I was gently shaken I opened my eyes to look into the face of the Archangel Gabriel, bending over me, cradling my head with his arms. What joy! I was in heaven with my own patron saint". What beauty! So that is how angles look. A lean face, hazel eyes and skin burned by the sun. Ah, yes I thought, heaven must also have a sun. But this heavenly vision was shattered when the angel spoke softly in Arabic, as he touched my gaping mouth with a wet cloth with drops of water trickling on my parched lips. I tried to speak but could not move my tongue made of lead. I still wanted to retain my heavenly vision but when he spoke again, wiping my face gently and massaging my forehead and temple, I

53

finally formulated the words 'water, water, angel of Allah", reverting to Arabic. The man laughed. "I am no angel, ya sheikh, I am a scout of the frontier force, a soldier of the king, and if I give you water, you will die – hush – only drops – gently, gently, do no swallow". He then cradled me in his strong lean arms "do not tremble for you are safe now. Our patrol spotted you by chance just as we were leaving. We have recently found many people fleeing Persian persecution dying like you in the wilderness".

"Water, oh angel Gabriel! Water." I pleaded. "I will give you a little laban (sour milk) and only drops of water. The sun will soon set and we will carry you back to the camp".

So I was not dead and the angel Gabriel was a solider of the Ghassanid king, but where were we? "How far was the Roman frontier?" The angel laughed. "You have crossed the frontier ya shiek, you are in Ghassanid territory under the protection of our king. May Allah give him long life".

I was silent. Had I lost my mind – did I cross the Euphrates in my sleep? How long have I been roaming the desert? But my thoughts were interrupted by a clamour of voices and I was surrounded by the full patrol on camels. "You found another one" they shouted. "Don't dilly dally Sirhan, let us carry him and go", but the angel Gabriel did not leave my side, giving me drops of laban, tenderly as a mother would give to a new born baby.

The patrol dismounted to have a look at the old man with the wizened shriveled face and his torn dirty tunic for I was in disguise. I had left my sacerdotal clothes in Hira. I could see the shock and pity on their faces, for I must have looked grotesque, blackened skin and bones, puffed, watery eyes. An argument followed as to who would carry me back to the camp, silenced by my angel Gabriel who gave the order, for apparently he was the chief of the patrol. He put me tenderly on the mount, for I had shrunk and my weight was negligible.

I have heard him give orders to those who would escort me for he felt as the Arabs did, that once he saved me he would be responsible for my life.

How beautiful were these youths, singing all the way the Bedouin monotonous solos, cries of war and serenades, proud of their service to the king who entrusted them with succoring the refugees who fled Persian torture and persecution. As my mind was cloudy I tried to remember the name of the king. It came back Harith bin Jabla, who established the Syriac church to which I belonged, whose tents were opened to dissidents and refugees, who incited terror in the Lakhmids of Hira and death in the hearts of the Persians whose arms gave them nightmares.

The youths tried to revive me by small talk as ordered by their chief, for they were afraid I would fall unconscious again and I was afraid of committing a solecism for their Arabic dialect was pure and a little different form the dialect of Hira.

I was dosing when I heard them laughing at my calling their chief Sirhan, the angel Gabriel. They esteemed I should have called him "Sarkis" the Arabicized name of St Sergius, the patron saint of the Ghassanids, but one of them cried "Our chief is no saint, ha ha" This aroused laughter and ribald comments and awoke me from my stupor and I said weakly "The angel Gabriel is my own patron saint" which silenced them.

In the camp they laid me on a carpet in a large tent, set aside for passing Bedouins and gave me some lentil soup, watched over by my angel Gabriel who came immediately to my tent on his arrival. When I tried to talk to him he put his hands on his lips saying I must not weary myself; for the present I must sleep. My sleep was feverish and delirious and was told that I was crying for a treasure, for the bundle on my back, which they set beside me saying "you are in a Ghassanid camp, ya sheikh and you and all your belongings are safe".

Time passed slowly and I was growing stronger every day, and to my amazement no one in the camp displayed any curiosity about me. No one asked about my name, or about my wandering in the desert. One evening when my angel paid me the usual visit after his tour of duty I put the matter to him. "You never asked me who I was". He smiled, surprised and said after a pause. "You speak Arabic, ya Shiekh, but you are a Syriac, for if you were an Arab you would not ask the question. A guest seeking refuge or just paying a visit would not be asked questions for three days, whatever his circumstances may be. He could be a murderer, a thief or a bandit. He may volunteer the information after three days if he so wishes, for it is an Arab's sacred duty to honour the guest and to give him full protection – his cause, or his enemies become our own – supposing that my father's assassin enters my tent, I am obliged to honour the rule and to protect him as my guest.

"It is time for me then to volunteer and to tell you my own circumstances" but the only surprise that he showed after I explained the theft and the flight was that I was an ecclesiast and as such he welcomed me again in the name of the king.

I then explained that I took the treasure to barter for my life and that as he saved my life the treasure should belong to him. I wanted to rise to open the bundle to explain to him the importance of the sacred treasure which holds within its folds the secret of riches beyond men's hopes, waiting to be reclaimed, but he restrained me and said "I saved your life as a solider of the king, it is therefore to the king that you must give the treasure". I was shocked. Your great king I will seek to give it to him by hand, for I must explain its significance." The resolve made me happy and made my recovery quicker. I asked daily about the whereabouts of the king who was moving from one frontier post to another and between his two capitals Jabiya and Jilliq. I was loath to leave the camp but I was aware that I was a burden on these brave soldiers who shared their meager returns with me, so I decided to go on to Edessa, to the Monophysite monastery of Mar Ephrem. It was perhaps not the wisest decision, but I had no other alternative.

My angel Gabriel arranged to send me with a detachment of the patrol that was going that way and came to bid me farewell but was indignant when I tried to give him some gold pieces. I embraced him with tears in my eyes as he left quickly saying "I leave you in God's keeping, ya shiek". The patrol left me in Edessa at the door of the monastery where I presented myself as the bishop of Hira, forgetting that I was in rags which resulted in insults and dismissal as an imposter and a charlatan. I thought it was curious that it was the garments that made a bishop out of me but I refused to budge. I sat at the gate screaming "here, come and see the bishop's ring on my finger". The head of the monastery heard my cries and sent for me where I identified myself to his satisfaction. I was sent to the bath and given sacerdotal clothes, after which I was invited to his table, but my stomach refused the rich food after the fare of the desert. For a few days I was treated as an honoured guest, but unlike the Arabs they plied me with their questions. "Where, when, how, what." Why did I want to travel to Jabiya and I had to repeat the litany, a Ghassanid solider saved my life and I wanted to give thanks to his king in person. Their curiosity was bottomless but sooner than I anticipated, the rumours of the robbery and my flight came with newcomers from Iraq so that everyone in the monastery knew that I pilfered the treasure.

The atmosphere changed into outright hostility with dirty looks and hushed silence as soon as I entered a room. My only hope was that they could not throw me out for I was a consecrated bishop. I began to make plans for running away for I saw menace and evil in their eyes. I studied carefully the location of the cells, the corridors, the stairs leading to the front garden and I made a plan for escape. From the store room I pilfered a thick tattered tunic worn by men in the street and divided the treasure into two parts, one in a sack attached to my tunic, the other under my cloak. In the hem of the tunic I sewed the remaining golden coins I had carried from Hira.

Soon enough one luckless night I was summoned to the chamber of the Chief Rabin where he sat with his deputy who, without an introduction, sternly and brutally asked me if it was true that I pilfered the Chaldean treasure from under the nose of its Nestorian guardians. "Do you deny that?" thundered the Chief

Rabin. "do you add deceit and lying to your thievery?" did you know that Edessa is full of fanatic Nestorian sleuths sent from Hira to recuperate the treasure". The Rabin was interrupted by his deputy whose eyes popped out as he cried 'Do you realize how you abused our hospitality?" Are you aware that you put this monastery in a dangerous position?" I was silent. The Chief Rabin continued "it is true that we owe you protection as you fled from Persian persecution, but we can only do so if you hand over the treasure right now".

Silence on my part edged them on and the deputy continued "We suspect your intention of handing over the treasure to the Ghassanid king, for we are aware that you were asking for his whereabouts. Speak, speak, for you are a man of the Church".

At that precise moment I broke down. I could not add lying to theft so I said "It is true. I intend to give it to those who saved my life, for my act to begin with was to barter the treasure for my life". On hearing this, they went mad and for men of the church they treated me to the foulest, most obscene oaths with an invective used only in the neighbourhood of brothels. They raised their voices almost menacing me physically shouting "You traitor, scum of the earth, you intend to give the Chaldean treasure to the Arab upstarts, A timeless treasure, to an Arab king?" This last assault made me so furious that I regained my strength and replied 'Speaking of upstarts, refer to yourselves, the

Ghassanid king is a descendant of the Sabeans, who were royal since unrecorded time. It is thanks to this king that you, an obscure priest, is sitting as a Rabin on a bishop's throne. It is this king who gave you your own church and the pleasure of reciting the liturgy in your language, instead of being Greek dogs and slaves".

The deputy rose from his chair, pointed his finger at me and said "you traitor, you forget our own Jacob Bradaeus". I laughed, "Would you tell me who fished this crude ascetic hermit from the wilderness and nominated him as bishop of Edessa? Didn't you know it was the king? True, he cannot enter this town but he is at large, consecrating priests all over the Orient, under the protection of the Ghassanid king. Tell me Rabin, who guarantees your safety in this hostile imperial town? And who opens his tents and palaces to receive the dissidents and the persecuted of your creed but who you call the upstart Arab king?"

Silence, I saw the old Rabin trembling with what emotion I do not know. 'Your reverence" he began, but after being called by all the dirty names that the Syriac language contains I could not believe my ears. "Your sins will be forgiven if you hand the treasure over for safekeeping'. I could not understand this sudden benevolence but the Rabin continued, "hand us the treasure and you are a free man". "Do I understand you correctly? Am I to consider myself your prisoner?" "Until you hand over the treasure you are – put it this way if you like – under our protection". I almost read their thoughts. They would take the treasure but the Nestorian sleuths would not know and would keep after me, a target scapegoat or a sacrificial lamb. Again I was silent for while the Rabin and his deputy were building castles in the air, dreaming of the golden future the possession of the treasure would give, a light shone in my brain, hypocrisy for hypocrisy, a lie for a lie, deceit for deceit. I resolved on running away this same night, but after a long pause I knelt humbly before the Rabin, kissed his hands, with tears streaming down my face. "My father, I have sinned and I humbly beg for your forgiveness. I will go now, wash my face, for my eyes are swollen and will come back with the treasure, hoping for your absolution".

They could not believe their ears for this act of complete volte-face, but I must admit that I was a good actor? "Ah" I said to myself "I should have chosen the career of acting instead of the Church".

They looked at each other and then at me, prostrate at their feet and thanked Alluhu loudly for my penitence. 'Go", the Rabin said 'Rise my son, the ways of Alluhu are mysterious, go and fetch the treasure, go in peace".

I rose and ran as soon as I got out of their sight. I put on the tattered tunic and the cloack over my clerical robes with the treasure underneath and left my belongings except for a hammer and a robe and walked down, according to the plan I had made.

I went straight to the front garden and hung the robe over a branch of an oak tree and dangled it outside the gate to give them the impression that I had jumped over the gate something I could not actually do. I then dropped myself in a hole in the ground near the gate which I had earmarked before and in which I had placed some dry branches. I jumped down, covered my head with twigs and waited. Then the reasonable interval of my absence passed, they panicked and searched my room, where everything was in its place. They called the guards and the domestics but they were not really disturbed for they knew there was no way to escape.

They divided themselves into two teams, one searching indoors, the other in the yard and garden. When the outdoor team saw the robe hanging on an oak branch they called the others, opened the gate and rushed outside to catch me on the road. I then raised myself out of the hole and while they were shouting and running in all directions I slipped through the gate and hid in a bend on the road while they were supposedly following my footsteps.

I waited throughout the night until they were exhausted calling invectives on my head and returned crestfallen and empty handed to the monastery.

I then walked without direction, thinking it was the third time I escaped death, the Persians of Hira, the desert, and ironically a Monophysite monastery, a creed which was the root of all my trouble, an escape in a divine plan. I then found myself in the midst of the quarter of the town where pimps, prostitutes and criminals held sway.

I was weary with swollen feet, puffed eyes and aches all over my muscles. I longed for a bed, for sleep, I walked around the area in the hope of finding an inn that was open. Finally I found an old building with a light in the first floor. I knocked on the door and a woman of no distinct age opened the door. I greeted her and she said 'What were you looking for, old man?" "Madame, I need shelter for the night. I can barely stand" I said as I stood, shivering and perspiring. "This is no inn, but you are sick and I cannot shut the door in your face" she said as she led me to a cell where I threw myself onto the wooden couch while she disappeared and came back with a bowl of soup. "Eat, and don't let the noises of your neighbours bother you". I thanked her but could not touch the soup. I tried to sleep but the clamour of voices speaking Arabic, Syriac and Greek was too loud and brutal that allowed no respite. There were girlish voices, meek and resentful and at times a girl was crying with pain and anguish. At last I must have slept and dreamed of beautiful half naked young girls parading languidly in the patio, but it was not a dream.

I screwed my eyes and there they were flesh and blood. When the woman from the night before whom I took for the housekeeper, came into my room she found me very ill. "Ah, no" she said 'I came to tell you that you must leave, but I see you are unable to move. You must be very ill, but I cannot call a doctor for I have no license for this brothel and he will report me to the authorities". "You said brothel" I gasped, and remembered the voices of the night and the half-naked girls. The woman was furious. "Yes, brothel old man. You did not expect to be in the king's palace did you? And if your morals bother you, you can leave right now". I apologized. "I thank you for giving me shelter. Actually this is the best place to be hiding. I am a man of sorrow. Two groups worse than your Roman authorities, are after me." I was sure that the Rabin would not dare inform the Roman garrison about my disappearance for they themselves were regarded by the authorities with suspicion, but that won't prevent him from pursuing me. It is indeed strange that both Nestorians and Monophysites are trying to corner me. "Madam" I said "I would be grateful if I could stay" and put two golden coins in her hand. The gold did the trick and she said "You can stay on condition that you keep to your room and not speak to the girls". I would be grateful if you could buy some medicine for me I said and put another golden coin in her hand. At the sight of more gold the old crone became amiable and started to straighten my bed with another pillow. She went off to buy the provisions and left me with the

65

atrocious pain I had felt in the desert and yet fate had conspired to save me by this fever, for no one will seek an old bishop hiding in a sordid brothel. As my fever diminished I asked the old crone to find out from the Arab merchants and soldiers frequenting the brothel the whereabouts of the Ghassanid king for I inteneded to travel to Jabiya in the Golan to see him as I had partially recovered.

One day she came to me smiling, with her hand stretched for one of my gold coins. "The king is going on his yearly pilgrimage to Sergiopolis to the shrine and tomb of St Sergius, the Ghassanid patron saint". I was overjoyed and asked her to find a caravan I could join. She did find one leaving in three days and so I started my preparation for the journey. I embraced the old crone as I said farewell, crying Hallelujah at last. I am unable to recount the horrors of that journey, with bandits, hunger and disease, for by the time we reached Sergioplis I was already half dead, when kind fellow travelers deposited me at this hostel. I already wrote of how I missed the king. Alas, alas I have no strength to follow him again. I am drained of all emotion and cannot leave this bed. But why on earth I refused to go with the guards at the palace gate who offered to take me to the Ghassanid Madafa, where I could have a bed and food for free. I moaned and groaned on the bed from which I knew with a sudden clarity that I would never get up again.

I cursed my-self and my fate aloud and I was unaware that my cries of pain were heard all over the hostel. One night a timid young man stood at the door and identified himself as Behnam, a monk form the Mar Murkus monastery in Jerusalem who was on a pilgrimage to St Sergius and offered his help. I asked him to come in and he immediately raised my pillows and made me sit on the bed which enabled me to breathe. He then went to the kitchen and brought some rice and beans and forced me to eat, but my situation was deteriorating fast and Behnam with an unlimited compassion nursed me day and night, with a devotion that was filial. I could have been his father. He brought me a physician whom he paid from his own pocket and refused stubbornly my golden coin. I guessed what the doctor told him, that it was too late and was not assured by his smile and denials.

Between the bouts of delirium when he sat on my bed I told him about the theft of the treasure, my flight in the desert and the second flight from Edessa and the horrors of the brothel. As I went on and on he became gentler and more compassionate and sometimes I caught the shadow of a tear on his cheek. I moaned and groaned about not giving the treasure to the king. He tried to ease my pain by giving me the illusion of a cure, and that I would soon find the king. He told me tales to relieve my pain and when I dazed I heard him singing to me a sad song almost like a lullaby.

One evening when I was short of breath I called him to my bedside and asked him to listen carefully to a request that I would put to him reluctantly for I had no other choice. I held his wet hands in mine and told him that I knew with a sure knowledge that I would never leave this bed and that I had failed to fulfill the mission I had undertaken to hand over the Chaldean treasure to the Ghassanid king as a token of gratitude but I will entrust him with the treasure, to hand over to the king. Behnam was grieved and shocked. "My father", he said "You overestimate my power. This is an impossible mission which I cannot do. I am a simple poor monk in a small monastery and do not have the freedom to travel to seek your king. What you ask is beyond my physical and mental resources. You know, father, I am willing to lay my life down for you but how can I undertake a task beyond me and which I cannot fulfill?"

I ignored his protest but he kept repeating. "How will I, a poor monk from Jerusalem, find the king of Ghassan". Again I ignored his objections until he asked me 'What if the king is dead, or I am dead". I then told him that if the king is dead, the treasure must go to a direct descendant and that if he did not deliver the treasure in his lifetime he must hand it over to his superior in Jerusalem and ask him to take a vow that he would deliver the treasure to a direct Ghassanid descendant. Behnam smiled and cried "Reverend Father" he said 'you are asking me something beyond my means or ability". But, feeling the end I became heartless and cruel, forcing the poor monk to vow on the Holy book and repeat the promise on a piece of the Holy cross encrusted in the cross I always wore around my neck. Alluhu, Alluhu, I cried in extreme agony. I added another sin to the one of theft. I threw a burden on a poor simple monk which I myself could not do. I knew that I charged him with an impossible mission and left him no choice to refuse but I also knew that this simple pure soul would keep the vow and the promise.

I am too feeble to write any more, Alluhu, I give thanks that in Behnam I found an unconditional filial love. It will be done.

I put the account of the bishop of Hira down, dazed, fascinated, shocked and amazed. "What does the ridiculous vow a dying bishop forced on a simple monk 1400 years ago have to do with me" I asked. My mind raced in circles as follows "A Monopysite bishop flees from Persian persecution in Iraq, steals an ancient sacred treasure guarded by the rival Nestorians, helped by the Ibad, the Christian Arab community of Hira, a theft which he justifies as a means to save his life and decides to give the stolen treasure to Ghassan, as a token of gratitude, fails and lays the burden on a monk of Jerusalem!!".

True, the treasure was not named in the account but I think I have an intelligent guess by elimination. It could not be an icon, a relic of a saint, a piece of the cross, or possibly the holy grail, for none of these could be divided in two. The idea of the Holy Grail, the cup that Jesus drank from during the last supper fascinated me as the last supper was held in the upper room of the Mar Markus Monastery, coincidence oblige, food for thought. Could it be a royal crown, but breaking a crown in two is not feasible. This leaves jewellery and gold, not likely either. I was almost sure it was a manuscript, an old manuscript that could be split.

The Ghassanid connection was the only reason I could see for my call because of an old traditional claim of my clan, an assumption built on oral tradition which could be only moving sand.

My fascination was rising with these Syriac monks who were glorifying a language that was almost dead but was once upon a time the language of the civilized world and reviving an ancient civilization with a two-faced god who once monopolized international inland trade and on adopting Christianity sent their missionaries to China and India where their creed has taken roots until today.

The fossils, as I once called them, were throbbing with life...

Chapter IV
A Sufi in Mamluk Street

The bishop's account set strange images whirring in my brain. I had no rest, my curiosity was only partially assuaged by the saga and yet the bishop's troubles and grievances became my own. I was possessed. "Beware", I said to myself "This is becoming an unhealthy obsession, an addiction, but soon enough a reaction followed and a kin of revulsion overcame me for I was being dragged into a foreign world – the world of modern Syriacs with their national aspiration and the world of ancient Syriacs with their cults but above all, that of the Chaldean seers with their magic and superstitions. I must pull out of all this before it becomes too late, but then it is too late already and I am up to my ears with only a semi-understanding of events. I must revert back to my normal life. What irony! As if my life had any semblance of normality with check-points and dividing metal walls, and on top an exclusion from the magic Medina of my childhood – my city, for the fifteen minutes from my village to Jerusalem needed a permit and oh, the ways of getting the permit and the days of waiting are too painful to recall.

I needed a change for I was sick of the treasure, the Aramean past and present, their past persecution and their present aspiration. In fact a visit to my friend in Khaski Sultan (I call Mamluk street) is due to my need for the Arab Jerusalem I knew and my instinct of sane self-preservation. I actually ran all the way bumping into walls and pedestrians until, breathless, I arrived at the crumbling ruin that was once upon a time a Mamluk palace. I ran from the dingy courtyard up the open stairs to his *Illiya,* a small upper room at the top of the house with a crudely painted dome.

My friend saw me from the small window overlooking the Aqsa mosque, climbing the stairs as he stood at the door. "Welcome, a thousand welcomes, what great event brings you to my door, panting like a horse? Come in, you must be in trouble. Have they finally got you?" My friend, who had come lately out of prison, saw everything in that light, Yes, I am in trouble, but I cannot tell you about it. Maybe later. Let me first rest my aching bones".

"Coffee, coffee without sugar" he shouted as he thrust his head out the window to his youngest sister playing in the courtyard.

We drank coffee silently then he said out of the blue "You know that at whatever hour you come, you will find me in this cell". "Of course I know. I saw your metamorphosis into a recluse". I did not elaborate for my friend, before he lost his job, was the editor of a well-known journal. The paper was closed by the Israelis on the pretext that it harboured what they called terrorists, but who were in reality young journalists who dared report facts about the occupation for which they were dismissed and imprisoned for inciting violence. My friend was the last of the group to come out of prison two years earlier, a changed man, a recluse, a mystic, a Sufi, for as he told me "What saved me from loneliness, wretchedness and revolt against injustice were the Sufi poets, for what other than poetry can save a soul from the degradation and humiliation of a prison?" As a passionate lover of Sufi poetry I rejoiced at this and our meetings were such joy as he read to me his favourite poems and I recited mine.

I told him I had a surprise for him, for I discovered a little stanza in the newspaper which was part of a long poem by the Sudanese poet (Faituri) who lives in Tunis and whose Sufism, neither of us was aware of. When I recited the poem he was so enchanted he got up and danced whirling like a dervish for the words were pure music to his ears. When he sat down I gave him a copy of the verse. As he began to make more coffee over his little stove, we chanted the verses together:

"In the presence of my beloved longing overwhelmed me

I gazed without a face and danced without a leg

I raised my banners high and my drums filled the sky

My love annihilates my love and my annihilation is submersion

Truly I am your adorer but also the sultan of lovers!"

We repeated the words dreamily, drunk with their music, until he stopped and said "I will not ask you what is wrong, but you look as if you have been struck by thunder and lightning. I laughed, for how could he know that I was in contact with the world of Hudded, the god of thunder and lightning. I just said "I see you have become a clairvoyant". "You could at least tell me what troubles you – as you often did in the past' he pleaded. I so longed to unburden myself and to tell him about the nightmare I was going through. But instead I started to ask him about the Syriacs of Jerusalem which irritated him. "You know Zuhra" he said 'with you I was hoping to talk of beauty which uplifts the spirit of the peace that only comes with Sufi meditation, but I see that you are still overtaken by irrelevant trifles. "Hey, hey" I screamed at him. "I only asked you a question. The Syriacs or as we call them the Siryan are part of our society. "Ah", he said, 'I was hoping that this evening you will soar above all those

74

things". "Stop it" I said cynically "to arrive at this state I need to go to prison first". And we both laughed. "Ah yes, it was when I reached the depths of humiliation and degradation inflicted upon me that I saw the light. I began to meditate. But Zuhra, I am still on the ground, my climbing the ladder is slow; I have not experienced the ecstasy the Sufis talk about. I still have not thrown my bonds of attachment. "Oh please, don't throw away your friends" I pleaded "don't cut me off like a discarded object – I am so afraid for you". "Afraid of what, Zuhra?" he asked impatiently 'I fear peoples' reaction, some of our friends will confuse your mystic state, with the occult or other fringe beliefs". "That" he said, "is not my concern. I wish I could explain to you, but words fail me. My inner sense of peace, my joyful stillness is beyond the busy minds of our friends. Your fear that I will discard you is utterly absurd. I am always there if you need support. I nodded gratefully and stood up to look from his window and said 'How lucky you are to live in Jerusalem" "Yes, yes, Zuhra. This city with all its layers of the past, all its veils is conducive to Sufism. Look beyond at the cells surrounding the Aqsa, al-Ghazali lived in one of them during the Crusades, but I see a question in your eyes".'Yes", I said. "I repeat my question about the Syriacs of Jerusalem". He laughed? "You do insist. The Syriacs are not many and they are assimilated with us. They speak Arabic, share our life and culture. Their language is preserved in the church, but some old people still speak Syriac. They are no

75

different from us". "You forget" I said "that most Palestinians, as well as Syrians and Lebanese, are descendants of the mixture of Canaanites and Arameans who spoke Syriac until the Arab conquest.They were Islamised and Arabicized, without any offense intended, many family names in Palestine are Syriac – your family included". He laughed loudly "Please do not say that to my family who have invented a tree which takes them back to Hijaz and to Quraysh – by Allah I should know by now your obsession with ancestral roots and genealogy". "I cannot help it" I said. Genealogy is an ancient Arab science and it is embedded in my genetic makeup". "So this is the new line, first the Syriacs, then the genetic makeup,'a surprise upon surprise'. We laughed, relaxing in the comfort of our childhood memories and the ridiculous tales of our respective families. In our immersion into old things I somehow regained my tranquility, if not normality, in an Arab Jerusalem, familiar and beloved. My friend insisted I stay for supper. I accepted on condition that he talk to me of Ibn al-Arabi, the great poet and Sufi he was studying and who was beyond my comprehension. Meanwhile, I telephoned my family and my cousin who lives in Jerusalem, to warn her not to close the outer gate of her house because I was intending to spend the night with her. I then settled on the divan, while my friend shouted from the window that we needed two narghiles (shiseh). I protested, but he said I must try. After the two trays of a delicious supper, followed by the shiseh I started quizzing him about Ibn al-Arabi, the alpha and omega of Sufism, of whom I only knew the exquisite poetry. I taunted him for being a student at his age for he was not only a serious student of Ibn Al Arabi, he was studying ancient Greek at the Dominican school in Jerusalem. "Zuhra" he said with reproach in his voice "the world is not shaped according to your moods and whims, studying Greek is a joy, compatible with studying Sufism". I apologized, telling him I was jealous for I would have liked to do the same. "You know that I am only a novice, the path is long, the Sufi love of poetry which you so much like, is not meant for humans, it is for Allah and the desire for union with him". "I do not agree" I said. Love for a man or a woman can be a way to Allah". We were silent except for the gurgle of the water in his shiseh. I stopped trying and threw the pipe away. The aroma bothered me, for my over sensitivity to bad and noxious odours was a malaise and I dreamt of a world of heavenly aromas. "Another new theme of yours; more and more rubbish" he said gleefully. "I note that when you are emotionally disturbed you speak rot". "To think" I said, sarcastically "my cat sim-sim is higher on the evolutionary scale than you, for she knows people by their odour". "Zuhra" he said sternly "I wish you could spill out what's bothering you. What is the secret? What mystery are you hiding?" I laughed. "Here is my secret – don't you know Ibn Al-Arabi on odours? It is he who said that the best odor is the embrace of a lover and didn't you know that the prophet loved three things in the world, one of them is perfume[1]. You know of course that he hated the smell of garlic, and according to Ibn Al-Arabi, "angels are harmed by bad odours. So there". Thus, my friend, humbled and sheepish went to his bedside table and opened a booklet and started to read:

He praises me

I praise him

He adores me

I adore him

At times I avow him

At times I deny him

He knows me

I deny him

I know him and testify him"

"Stop, stop" I said, "not before you listen to this"

I have two faces

He and I

I am not him

---

1   Ibn al-Arabi, Fusus al-Hikam, Algiers 1991, pp. 197, 203.

I am I" [1]

I snatched the booklet out of his hand and read like prayer "His mercy engulfs all things great and small'[2] "but I want you to explain to me his meaning beyond the veil of his words". "That is not easy" he said. "Mystical thought lies at the opposite extreme of rational thought and the mystic experience is hard to put into words, it is an overwhelming sense of being at one with the universe or with God[3]. Ibn al Arabi was pantheistic, God is everything and everything is in god. Man has all the attributes of a miniature universe, and in him are all the elements, and man is the eye of al-Haq (Allah) as the pupil is to the eye of man. "Stop, stop, I cannot follow you". "Of course you cannot for Ibn Al-Arabi has chosen emotion, intuition, and imagination instead of analytic reason, for reason cannot express what is beyond logic and analysis. There are steps, grades and conditions that a Sufi follows and I cannot explain. You know, Zuhra, It is best not to speak of these things. Silence is deeper than speech. There are things which one cannot speak of, for when you open the mouth knowledge vanishes as darkness when the light appears". "Yes", I said "the

1   Ibn al Arabi, op cit, pp. 40 ,41.
2   Ibid, p. 79
3   Paul Davies, The Mind of God, London 1992, pp.226-227.

Sufi path is long and hard, and with all my love of Sufi poetry I am very, very, far from it".

The night drew on. It was getting late and my friend would not hear of my going alone in the dark alleys of the city to Sheik Jarrah. We hardly spoke as he accompanied me for the shadow of Ibn Al-Arabi was between us.

I woke up late the next morning, fortified by my evening of Sufism. I decided to have a final show-down with Abouna. I was not going to go back to my village to await his call. There were too many unanswered questions. I therefore walked down from Sheik Jarrah to Damascus gate and from there traversed the old city to the monastery. What worried me was that if something happened to Abouna I would remain in the dark forever. Meanwhile, there was something uncanny, unhealthy, about the whole affair; a Christian bishop who is a devotee of Huddud, a monastery in which a young monk recites psalms to the two faced God and yet another bishop who, 1400 years ago stole a treasure and pretended he was not a thief. All this, I said to myself, is in the name of what? Religious zeal that made a man of the church fleeing persecution become a thief? Or does the aim of a national revival of a people forgotten by history and on the verge of extinction make Abouna a secret devotee of the ancient gods?

This time, I said to myself, I must know the truth – or the many truths – for in every instance when I come to a precise point Abouna turns my questions and never answers them. It must be a kind of hypnosis that he exercises over me with those half blind eyes with heavy lids.

Abouna expressed no surprise at my impromptu visit. He seemed to be waiting to hear my comments on the account I read. I told him that I surmised that the treasure was a sacred manuscript pertaining probably to Chaldean magic and not, as I thought before, a treasure of gold and precious stones. As to my presumed role built on a false premise, that is the Ghassanid connection, is purely a claim without proof. "Hem, hem" Abouna said "not bad! But didn't you feel there was something missing in the account or that he carried his mystery till the end. For even on his death bed he did not reveal the truth". "Abouna", I said, "what more could he tell and what could he hide?" "He was hiding his greed, for he kept repeating that he stole the treasure to save his life but that is only half the truth". "Abouna", I said trying to corner him. "Do not speak to me of veils, mysteries and half-truths". 'you, my child have been intrigued by our calling it the "treasure" and you have been guessing at whether it could be a treasure of money and jewelry that the bishop stole. You were not far from the truth, for it was well known in Hira that the manuscript indicated the place of the treasure of Alexander the Great, the

81

treasure above all treasures which wet the appetite of many seekers, but the fact was only known by the few in the priestly order. The story as it was told to me was that the Chaldean priests of Babylon who were prophets and seers foresaw the imminent death of Alexander in the city of Babylon as they arranged a procession to meet him on his approach to the city. The priests were shocked to see the youthful king exhausted for the rude campaign in India and the death of his friend Hephastion had taken their toll. The high priest pleaded with the king not to enter Babylon for there he would meet with disaster for the priest saw the beautiful youth surrounded by darkness. Alexander was adamant. He had enjoyed the city before he left for Bactria and India and dreamed of his return to this paradise amidst the hardships and perils of the war. The exquisite luxuries which the beautiful city offered were to his taste, the lush gardens, the temples, the baths, the food and the wine. For him Babylon offered more than Dion and Pella in his own Macedonia or Ephesus and Aspindos, the Greek cities on the coast of Asia Minor could ever offer. It had a subtlety, a finenness, for it was more ancient than the Greek cities and was more sensual and voluptuous, and Alexander needed all that to relax". Abouna paused, asked for coffee and then continued "You are a student of history, my child, but you cannot compare the glory of a decadent Babylon with what Paris, London and New York have to offer today. It went far beyond them in all things that gave pleasure and joy. So Alexander

with all this precognition would not listen to the
Chaldeans and he entered the city with all the pomp,
the processions, the dance, the music, that was his due.
It did not take long before Alexander was ravaged with
fever and no treatment could be of avail. When they
finally moved him from the city and laid him in a
pavilion on the Tigris, his condition worsened and he
knew that he would die. So before he lost the power of
speech he sent for the Chaldean high priest of Bel and
signaled he wished to see him alone.

"You see, Father, your prophecy was correct and
I am dying, but as you foresaw my death I want you to
foresee my succession" Alexander said wearily in a
low voice, signaling to the priest to come nearer.

The high priest was grieved beyond words at the
withered body of the golden youth, who some
worshipped as a god. "Do not hesitate, you were
outspoken when I was alive. Now that I am half dead,
you must tell me what you see" Alexander said. The
priest closed his eyes and said after a long interval,
"My lord, you will have a son who will rule.
Alexander smiled, for he knew that Roxane was with
child, but he murmured 'What chance will the poor
orphan have amidst all these sharks". The priest said
nothing. "Speak, what is the fate of this future king of
Macedonia?" "I regret, my lord, I cannot see further
my powers are limited". The priest lied, for he foresaw
the disastrous future of the infant, but would not
distress the father on his death bed. Alexander spoke

again. "I will entrust you with my treasure, all the jewels from India and all the money I have to hand over to my son on his majority. The treasure must be kept from the eyes of my greedy generals who will divide the empire between them, but the treasure is for my son" and he pointed to a wooden box beside his bed. "Tonight at midnight the only two servants I trust will carry the box to your residence. I do not trust any of my courtiers, generals and friends who surround me, neither do I trust my servants. One of them slipped poison into my wine and they are all waiting for my death". Drained and exhausted, Alexander raised his hand in farewell. The priest bowed, knelt down and kissed the shriveled hand of the king and left with tears in his eyes. The next day Alexander lost the power of speech and could only return the greeting of his bereaved weeping soldiers, around his bed in farewell, by raising his eyebrows with a shadow of a smile to the brave men who had followed him to the end of the earth.

I was so moved by Abouna's tale and like Alexander's soldiers I had tears in my eyes. The tragic end of the godlike youth held the imagination of generations for a long time after his death. Abouna continued, "The high priest of Bel hid the treasure but on the approach of his death, before Alexander's son reached maturity he put down in numbers in the prophecy the place where the treasure was safely hidden. "you know, my child, how the Assyrians and

Chaldeans deified numbers and even gave the moon and the sun a number. The deciphering of these numbers is given only to the few adepts but some say that the high priest also left a diagram of the place".

"You mean to tell me, Abouna, that since the 4th century BC until the 6th century AD, for a thousand years, the treasure lay untouched in its hiding place and that none of the Nestorian and Chaldean adepts who kept the manuscript could find it?"

"This is the current theory that no one ever found the treasure and now you could see that the motive of the bishop who pilfered the manuscript was not only to save his life but also the treasure. "But, Abouna" I interrupted, "the bishop knew that he could never go back to Hira". "Yes, that's true, but it seems that he thought that he could do it through a third person". "No, no" I objected, this thesis does not fit his desire to hand it over to the Ghassanid king".

"My dear child, Ghassandis invaded the Lakhmids of Hira several times and who knows if the bishop thought that one day they would occupy Hira and eject the Lakhmids – and lo – the treasure could be sought then".

"This is too far-fetched, Abouna" I objected. "What I think is that the bishop, desperate of ever returning to seek the treasure, ensured that by giving it to the Ghassandis, no one would ever lay hands on it, neither the Nestorians of Hira nor the monophysites of Mar Ephrem".

"We are all in the world of hypotheses and conjecture my child, perhaps if the treasure was found in the thousand years that separated the death of Alexander from the flight of the bishop of Hira, it would still be lying in its tomb sealed forever by the priest of Bel. But remember that the legend of the treasure was alive in Hira, in the time in which it was stolen and that the thief did not see fit to mention it in his account". Hira, as you know, is very close to ancient Babylon".

"What happened to the monk Behnam who brought it to Jerusalem?" I asked. "Ah he went through Calvary" said Abouna "for he discovered the loss of half the manuscript only after the funeral and as he could not report the loss of stolen goods he could not get any help to look for the thieves, although he was sure they were the agents of the monastery of Mar Ephrem of Edessa who must have followed the bishop, but he could not rule out the possibility of Nestorian sleuths from Hira who were on the trail of the bishop since his flight, but whoever stole the manuscript did not realize that he had only half the treasure. Behnam, distraught, sewed the other half inside his tunic, paid the hostel with the last pieces of gold and left for Jerusalem.

In the monastery he made himself a nuisance for he pestered the Rabin about the promise and the vow he made to deliver the manuscript to the Ghassanid king. The Rabin who loved Behnam like a son, indulged him but refused to comply with the promise made to the dead bishop before scholars could decipher the manuscript. For although the existence of the manuscript was known, no one in the 6th century knew its contents, which went back to a time immemorial.

Behnam moped, cried, groaned and recounted to the other monks the last days of the dying bishop and how he kept repeating "the treasure drenched with blood", the blood of all those executed in Hira, the two acolytes who died in the deserts and his plea for Alluhu to forgive him for the wrong turn his life had taken.

The Rabin's heart melted at the pain of the young monk, but he could not possibly accede to his wish to travel to find the Ghassanid king before the document was interpreted. Behnam sickened and refused to eat or take medicine or join in the life of the community until he was on the point of death a tortured soul for he did not keep the promise that in reality was forced upon him. To appease him and possibly to bring him back to life, the Rabin wrote a decree to be enforced by all his successors on the bishop's throne, to adjure to deliver the manuscript to a descendant of the Ghassanid king, only when two conditions were met; the recuperation of the lost half and the interpretation by scholars of its contents for it contained, besides the religious texts, prophecies that foretold the future, and was full of numbers, diagrams, charms, and a great deal of astrology written presumably by Berossus the famous priest of Bel at the end of the 3rd century BC". I jumped from my chair. "You said Berossus – the priest who retired to the island of Cos – where people flocked to hear his prophecies?" "Yes, my child, Berossus himself who translated Chaldean astrology text books into Greek".

"Abouna; your Rabin must have been a vicious, spiteful hypocrite, for the two conditions he put are impossible to realize, which makes his decree nil. "You are intolerant my child, the decree was a balm to the dying Behnam to whom it was read, for he had lost his sight and moved his lips to speak but no words came out of his throat but he groped and gestured to kiss the hand of the Rabin with a smile like a flood of light, and he died in peace".

Abouna waited for my comments but all I could say in a tone of sarcasm was "I presume the decree is still in force". "Ha, ha, ha, finally my child we come to the point. The decree was dormant until I activated it. It is your turn to play cat and mouse with me for you surely know that your presence here means it was activated and now allow me, my child, to boast and inflate my ego a little for we all need that don't we? Let me take you back to 1719, when the monastery

88

came back to life and the then bishop Abdel Ahad Bin Fentah, gave his attention to rebuilding and reorganizing the library of the monastery with special attention to the manuscripts. Until that date nothing was done about the manuscript or the decree, the excuse was the unfulfilled stipulations. When I became bishop I spent a great deal of time studying the ancient manuscripts, amongst which I came upon the first half of the treasure and the decree which I felt bound to honour, but I soon realized that this small, poor monastery could not do it alone. However the time was ripe, for it came to my knowledge through many sources that the lost half of the manuscript was in Edessa and so I took the unprecedented step of putting the whole question officially to the committee of Nine in Sweden.

The Committee gave the manuscript which I carried with me to Stockholm to Syriac scholars to study, but they could partly decipher its contents. The report they made was sensational, shook the scientists in the Committee to such a degree that two of them resigned, for the report indicated prophesies that have mainly come true and this first half went up to World War II which it described in detail".

Abouna stopped for more coffee, while I was saying to myself 'Allah, Allah, another mystery". Aloud I said "What committee was this?" He replied that it was a committee composed of three Chaldeans, three Assyrians and three Syriacs who work for the preservation of the Syriac, Aramean language and for the renaissance of the three branches of one people". "I suppose it was one of these secret societies working underground" I said, piqued, for secret sociètiès are anathema to me. "The Committee of Nine is above ground! Luckily it was very interested in the manuscript as one of the oldest vestiges of our past and glorious civilization. It will accordingly finance its recuperation and after that it will assign for the research on the manuscript and its interpretation by the best national scholars. Luckily we have enough astronomers, linguists, historians and scientists who are in the Diaspora and finally, they named me the coordinator and chief of the project. I hope this answers your questions".

"Yes and no" I said. "There are too many facets to your saga. I presume I am here because you know that my clan is said to be Ghassanid, but it is only a claim, there is no proof whatsoever". He shook his head several times and then combed his beard before he answered me. "You are too quick for me. I wanted to prepare you psychologically for a fantastic story. You accused me in words and thought of being too much a man of the church and a man who worships the pagan past of his people. I am also a Syriac nationalist, a nationalism which includes the two other Syriac speaking people, the Assyrians and Chaldeans". I interrupted, 'you forget the Maronites of Lebanon. They also preserve your language in their liturgy".

"Tut, tut, these people are arrogant, they don't want to call themselves Syriacs which they are, and have invented for themselves fantastic ancestors, the Phoenicians. What absurdity when all geographical Syria has the Canaanite/Phoenician human base and when some of these Maronites are Arab tribes Christianized long before Islam". "But surely, Abouna, you have other hidden motives than preserving the language," I said. "Yes, yes, my child, I hate to tell you we have our extremists and our zealots who speak of a national home in their ancient land, Beit Naharin – a vague appellation which includes Iraq and Syria and southern Turkey, formerly north Syria, but the rest of us know it is only a chimera and all we hope for is the revival of our heritage". "What? Abouna, you realize you want part of the Arab world for a home, the words "national home" give me a chill, one is enough!" he shook his head. "No, not even the zealots have gone that far. We really are assimilated in the Arab fabric, our daily language is Arabic, our poets write in Arabic, but let me finish my story, you interrupt so much that I lose the thread".

I apologized, knowing that he was pleased to have an auditor as he hastily continued his monologue. "Before I put the question to the Committee of Nine, I had to have the approval of our patriarch the head of the Syriac church, whose seat now is in Damascus, after the French handed Antioch, the ancient seat, to the Turks. The patriarch was pleased with my initiative

91

and recommended me to the Committee, who received me with honour in Stockholm, in honouring Jerusalem. The thorny part was handing the manuscript on recuperating the second half to a Ghassanid descendant. Most members were head against the idea of an Arab holding a precious part of our heritage and that because of a promise to a dying man so many centuries ago. I stood firm, I insisted that a promise is a promise, a vow is still a vow and that in the final analysis, Mar Murkus owns half the manuscript and in case of their refusal it will be kept under lock and key in our library. Finally a compromise was reached. They agreed to hand the manuscript symbolically to a Ghassanid but that the manuscript would remain in the library of our monastery. I insisted that the Ghassanid would have the power of veto in case of publication. They, however, insisted that I give them an authentic Ghassanid who would be charged with recuperating the manuscript, for it is easier for an Arab to move around Edessa and the surrounding area than a Syriac. I did not agree to this last point for it is a risky and dangerous job. The most difficult point they raised was to find a Ghassanid of the blood". I was aghast, shocked into mutism while Abouna was shouting with glee. "Their decision was a vindication for the bishop of Hira, for Behnam and my-self," he said with his face beaming with beatitude.

"There is a fly in your ointment, Abouna" I said maliciously "for how on earth could you prove that anyone is a Ghassanid?" "That is the big surprise my child". "Again you are playing cat and mouse. You still do not trust me" I said. But from the way Abouna's lips twitched I knew that he was hurt. "I was congratulating myself on your calm reaction my child but I was cheated by your apparent tranquility". "The tranquility Abouna is a result of Sufi poetry which acts as a catharsis to my troubled soul".

"Alluhu, so you are a Sufi adept, so was I a long, long, time ago. I am still a lover of Arabic poetry, though now I read less as my sight is failing". "How you amaze me, a bishop of Christ, priest of Huddud and a Sufi lover, who are you Abouna?". "Tut, tut" he said, pleased with himself for my inflation of his ego always worked. "Don't exaggerate, my child, each of us has many facets. We are like a prism that reflects the light, some, alas, live and die with their facets closed, their prism unlit, and some have the capacity of being a multitude in one, but I must tell you about my Sufi experience. One day in our ancient land I was visiting a friend who had studied in the West, a relentless lover of music. I hardly put my foot in the room when he clutched my shoulders and said "Listen to this music and tell me what it is". The music and the chant were superb, celestial and when it ended he turned to me as I said "This is the traditional Greek Orthodox Church music and chorus which they say was the old Greek chant for Apollo. It is Greek, pagan turned into Christian". My friend laughed loud and long as he said "This is the chant of the Turkish Dervish Mawlawy order."

"What!" I cried "The Turks took over the church music too!" "Open your mind" my friend said, "Sufism is universal, the essence is the same in all religions, the mystic longing for the union with God is one and indivisible whether it is in Christianity, Islam, Judaism or Buddhism and that my dear child is a lesson I never forgot".

"I am only a novice of Sufism through the exquisite poetry. I have a friend who came to Sufism through suffering and humiliation, the ways vary," I said. "Yes, the ways are many but the end is the same" Abouna agreed 'Now, we are far from our subject. You will soon be accusing me of the cat and mouse game" he said playfully. "For once, Abouna, please tell me the truth" I said sternly. "We have been turning around the subject but I am still in the dark, why me?"

Abouna sighed and groaned before he answered "The Committee of Nine wanted a woman to recuperate the lost half, because they thought a woman would be more discreet and less vulnerable than a man in evading pursuers, but I hesitate to tell you the rest because I do not necessarily agree with them, the woman had to be single, relatively young, versed in history of the east and of Ghassanid blood, but wait, my child, how can I say it" and he stopped, embarrassed "She must not have a partner or a lover

94

for he may be working for the other side" I jumped and stood up. "What is all this, pursuers, the other side, what other side?" I had by now lost my capacity for surprise. Abouna said in a tone of reciting a lesson. "The manuscript, or as they call it the 'Chaldean prophecy" is considered a national treasure by the present government of Iraq for they are the heirs of the Assyrians and Chaldeans, the government of Syria has a claim as the land of Aram and the cradle of the Aramean language and the Turks who occupy north Syria, our ancient land, know that the lost half is somewhere in Edessa and that it rightly belongs to them. European governments are interested in laying their hands on it for different reasons, for their universities with the departments of Aramaic studies and ancient history are clamouring for it for research but what's more, they were led to believe that the prophesies are accurate. Oh my dear child, they want to know what the future holds for all of us and they would stand at nothing to get a hold of the manuscript. Six governments are leading the search with their agents and spies in Turkey, Iraq, Syria, Britain, France, Russia and the United States of America. It is said that the prophecy foretells not only the end of our planet but the universe and they want to be the first to know".

"Allah, Allah," I said, so it is not magic medicine, religion or philosophy, nor is it charms and potions as I thought, but prophesies".

A long, heavy, unbearable silence followed, as I said in an afterthought. "You did not tell me my role in this esoteric mess and what made you sure that I am of Ghassanid blood."

Chapter V

Genetic Makeup

"For that you have to thank your genetic makeup" and Abouna smiled, speaking to me as if he were giving a toy to a child. "What, how?" I cried. Abouna now had the upper hand and was clearly enjoying himself. "If you would indulge an old man and promise not to interrupt I will tell you a tale. Once upon a time in the 6th century there was a Harith bin Jabla, king of Ghassan, head of a federation of northern Arab tribes, an ally of the Eastern Roman Empire, and a guardian of its frontier, and as such he was king of the Arabs and the Arameans in Syria. The term Aramean includes descendants of Canaanites and Phoenicians on the Mediterranean and dwellers of Assyria and Babylon, the Aramean natives of Syria were called Syriacs, or Siryan, who had assimilated the Canaanites and other inhabitants of Syria and were downtrodden under Byzantine heels. The Syriacs were orthodox like the Romans but of a different creed, Monophysitism, a belief in one nature of Christ, instead of two. Abouna paused, seeing me wiggling in my chair. "Patience, my child, you are bored because you know all this but you must allow me to do it my way". I apologized as he went on. "The Byzantines opposed our religious beliefs and despised us as their subjects, forgetting in their arrogance that we were heirs to an ancient civilization. In other words we were a species near extinction, almost wiped out of history when Harith bin Jabla took us to his heart, protected us from Roman persecution and established for us with the help of the empress Theodora, a national Syriac church which preserved our identity and our language in its liturgy, a church that I have the honor to represent. Harith and his descendants paid a heavy price for our protection for they clashed with the Orthodox ecclesia and imperium but Harith and his son Mundir gave us our brief golden age, but when the situation of the Ghassanids deteriorated we were without protection and persecution followed upon persecution. Our last known Syriac insurrection against the Romans was in the beginning of the 7th century (608) in Antioch. The Assyrians had uprisings in northern Iraq in 1920 and 1933. It is true that under the Arabs in the 7th century we recovered our religious freedom, however history passed us by until the atrocious massacres by Kurds and Turks after World War I and the exodus from our native homeland". Again, Abouna paused. "I repeated this forgotten history to explain to you why I chose to go through all this complicated affair of giving the 'prophecy' to a Ghassanid – not only because I wish to honour a promise, but because of this ancient debt that we owe to Ghassan.

In modern times the feeling for a national revival of a people without a homeland grew mainly in the Diaspora and resulted in societies springing up in exile. My personal and official involvement in this affair was when I discovered the first half of the neglected prophecy lying on the shelves of our library since the 18th century.

I already told you about my visit to Sweden when I put half the prophecy I carried from Jerusalem to the Committee who made a semblance of agreeing to my conditions, however they told me bluntly that the Ghassanid I designate must recover the lost half and above all to be of authentic Ghassanid blood. They calculated that this last stipulation was not possible, but they did not know the obstinacy of the humble servant of God sitting in front of you.

A pause for coffee and manna of heaven followed, after which Abouna continued. "My task was to find a man/woman of Ghassanid descent and so I began my discreet enquiry. I did not leave a stone unturned, I even called bona fide historians to help me find a Ghassnid. I was in despair until I came upon a very old man from Karak, living in misery in the Christian quarter of Jerusalem. He led me to your village which is luckily near Jerusalem and gave me the history of your clan which was always known as Ghassanids who migrated from Karak in the 16th century. I spotted you through a Syriac woman by the name of Um Mulki who did domestic work in your village, as a washerwoman. I thus knew you were single and had studied abroad. Other information followed, especially that you had no present involvement with a man". Abouna was embarrassed and I winced.

"But the snag was how I could prove that you were Ghassanid or that you would accept the role. We had you followed, and your psychological profile made by experts and you seemed to fit our requirements.

I trembled every time I was informed that you might be leaving and was desperate for a proof of your Ghassanid blood, but ah, my child, the ways of Alluhu are unfathomable. The miracle happened". "Abouna, Abouna" I teased him "you went through all this trouble without knowing whether I would accept the role you have assigned to me and which may not be to my liking, and you gave yourself the right to invade my life, my privacy and on top of all to rearrange my life! Abouna, this is scandalous". "Tut, tut, my child, we will see about that".

I was annoyed because he seemed so sure that I would accept. However he ignored me and continued. "One day a Western archaeologist was visiting the church while I happened to be there and put to me some questions about the inscription. He told me he had just come from Jordan, where he visited a friend of his, a famous Franciscan archaeologist priest who had just discovered in the obscure village of N'tl , near

Madaba, two churches, one of them a sepulchral church for the high ranking phylarchs from Bannu Ghassan, which he dated to the first half of the 6th century.

In spite of my heavy feet I jumped from my chair on the news and pestered him for details. I asked him whether they found bones and he answered a little annoyed "What would a tomb contain, if not bones?" I persisted by asking him what made the archaeologist think they were Ghassanid tombs, and he explained to me that the inscriptions had Ghassanid dynastic names, besides the area of Balqa in Jordan was known since ancient times as the seat where the Ghassanids first settled in immigration to Syria from Yemen.

My visitor wondered at the joy I showed about the tombs and probably thought I was one of those priests unhinged by their profession and confinement to a small monastery, but indulged me by telling me all he knew about the dig.

As soon as he was gone I set the stones rolling. You would be surprised my child that an old priest like my-self is knowledgeable about new scientific discoveries and techniques. I immediately thought of the 'genes' as the solution!". After this gleeful boasting we had the right for another tray of coffee and sweets and he said teasingly, "if you are bored and tired I will stop here". "No, no, please go on" I pleaded. "I thought you would" and he continued. I set my plan and invited the Syriac priest in Amman to Jerusalem. I used my privilege as his chief and charged him with a secret mission to obtain one bone from the newly discovered tombs. The priest was reluctant and told me with indignation "Your reverence, I am a priest, not a tomb robber" but he executed his charge beautifully, as he moved from Amman to Madaba for a few days where he learned about the dig and found a Syriac among the workers to whom he gave some money and charged him with pinching a bone from the tomb or from the cabinet where the archaeologist kept the artifacts.

When the bone was sent to me I rejoiced but I had to have something from you to compare with the bone, obtaining blood was unthinkable but one of our young monks who had some knowledge about genes had read in a scientific journal about genetic tests and suggested that hair would do. So we found out that you had frequented a hairdresser in Jerusalem, in the past and that he still dyes your hair on your rare visits to Jerusalem. What luck! For there was a Syriac boy working in this salon and whom I called and gave your name and your description, from photographs in your file, and asked him to await your visit and to obtain some hair. He stopped, exhausted, took some water and asked for my comments. "Abouna", I said, "my only comment is that you have Syriacs everywhere, from tomb robbers, to hair dressers". He laughed and continued. "When we received a small cutting from your hair I sent it with the bone to the Committee of Nine, who would find the proper laboratory to undertake the examination". He stopped and said with a theatrical gesture "Guess what, my child, the result was positive you are a bona fide Ghassanid. Hallelujah! That is when you were accosted on the street"!

I was silent, overwhelmed overjoyed, that I was a true Ghassanid but I did not want to show this to Abouna, instead I pretended indignation. "You do all this in my back Abouna? It is outrageous". "Ha, ha" he laughed, "I knew you would be pleased". "Abouna", I said, "Now at last you will tell me what this great treasure manuscript contains that is so important". "Yes, yes, my child, there is however a fly in the ointment. The Committee informed me that they insist on your agreement which stipulates that the designated Ghassanid had to recover the lost prophecy. They have already set a large network of detectives in southern Turkey, but to our dismay, discovered that seven countries, including Turkey, have also put their agents in search of the prophecy".

"Stop, Abouna, count me out. I am not playing the game of a spy in competition with experienced spies from seven countries. Who do you think I am – Mata Hari? And how on earth did the seven countries know about the lost prophecy? It was all hush hush!" Abouna said, crestfallen. "There was a leak, either from this monastery, or from the offices of the Committee in Sweden".

He fell silent, for the request of the Committee that I undertake the search was against his wish and his better judgment. I felt bitter and cruel and I taunted him. "It is ironic, Abouna, that you found the Ghassanid but not the treasure. You are out of your mind to ask me to go to Turkey as a spy. This is the straw that broke the camel's back". My anger and fury rose. "You can tell your Committee of Nine, Ten or eleven to go to the nether land or to go to hell. This is foul play and I am not party to it". I got up and walked towards the door. The old man raised his hand and tried to get up but he wobbled and almost fell, so I had to stretch my hand to steady him as he said, 'you are free – free to leave, free to refuse, but before that let me at least tell you about the treasure. I owe it to you. I was keeping it till the end. Please take your seat and listen to me. It is the last request I ask of you". I returned to my chair, ashamed of my outburst, but still boiling with rage. "Since the beginning of time", Abouna said, the Babylonians who were later known as Chaldeans, practiced astrology and sooth saying. It was given to their wise men and to their astrologers to see in the stars. Each Chaldean generation had its visionaries and prophets who recorded what they saw first on cuneiform tables and then on parchment. In a later unknown age, Chaldean priests collected the vision and prophecies without any chronological order into one manuscript, that became known as the Chaldean prophecy. It included visions of the universe from the beginning of the creation until the end of time. The prophecies are mainly recorded in numbers, for the Assyrians and Babylonians believed in numbers, the moon for example, was number 30 and they also expressed these visions in symbols, for example, circles, triangle and in diagrams and figures and sometimes in ancient Aramaic texts. The prophets did not always understand the visions and expressed in symbols the strange things they saw. Can you imagine a man in let us say 500 BC, a technologically primitive man putting in numbers a modern airplane, radio or telephone and machines that are yet to come, that are still eons away in the future.

We know all this because scholars have partly deciphered the Jerusalem manuscript which dealt with the past, but the complete interpretation will take longer than the lives of scholars. It is beyond me to understand or describe the difficulties the scholars met, but it is uncanny the way these early prophets saw and put in symbols and numbers, the car, the airplane, the submarine, the tank. To the general surprise, the scholars found out the predictions recorded were machines, which are part of our present daily lives.

The prophecy deals not only with decades or centuries but in eons, which leads us to believe that the second half will accurately tell the future, especially how the universe will end.

It will tell us eon by eon what the future holds. It will probably give us blueprints for future machines, the coming technological developments – besides the coming upheavals, wars, and catastrophes. You will appreciate the impact such future visions will have upon the different countries, which will be competing to lay their hands on the blueprints of the future. Whoever finds the manuscript first will get the upper hand. But the Committee of Nine hopes to keep it in its hands – a very delicate and dangerous procedure and you my dear want to run away from the most interesting project this planet has ever known. It was given to you by the right of your birth to arbitrate on any decision the Committee takes with a right of veto as the symbolic owner. You have the world my dear child in your hands and you want to run away, when you are called to preside over the destiny of the treasure above all treasures. Do you still want to run away?

Silence, tears were streaming on my face. Abouna said humbly, "There is still time for you to reflect on all the consequences of your decision. Remember that you are free to say the great 'yes' or the great 'no' but once you accept, there is no turning back. I say this, my child, taking the risk of losing you and all the efforts and energy we put into finding you, but I tremble for your fragility, for your primeval innocence. I am overwrought, but I hope to hear your answer in three days, until then, farewell".

I admit that I was touched by the streak of humanity Abouna showed, although a little late, his calculation worked, for how could I refuse to seek a prophecy which foretells the end of the universe, and like a sleepwalker, drugged by strange dreams, hypnotized by the unknown I walked into the trap that Abouna had so carefully prepared.

On my return to the monastery I found the whole apparatus set for the voyage, for it seems they never envisaged my great 'no'. The briefing for the journey required that I stay in Jerusalem where they booked for me a room in the *Notre Dame* hotel, and an intensive course of spoken Turkish with a Syriac priest who had lived in Diyar Bakr was my daily fare. Besides Turkish I was instructed to study maps of Edessa (Urfa) and the surrounding area for it was surmised that the prophecy was somewhere there. I was given details of the spies that were or would be in the area for the same purpose, for ever since the news seeped out that Syriac scholars were studying the first part of the prophecy, all eyes were set on finding the other half.

I was instructed on how to elude those who would track me, befriend me or otherwise and was informed that four agents who would identify themselves by number 1,2,3, and 4 would be there to help me, two in the hotel in which I would be lodged, one in the souk (market) and one near the great mosque.

My cover was to travel to southern Turkey for a non-governmental organization on a sociological project in Edessa (Urfa), which entailed research on women in various ethnic groups.

They asked for my passport in order to get a Turkish visa and handed me an elegant Fendi travel bag, for they were catering to my taste and my fondness for luxury goods, which was not surprising since they knew everything about me. The elegant bag had money, dollars, Euros and Turkish pounds, generous sums from the Committee of Nine which was funded by rich Syriacs and Chaldeans, mainly in the United States of America, with maps, brochures on southern Turkey and the number of the four agents with a name. No 1 was shoes, No 2 laundry, No 3 spice and No 4 books. I was allowed one suitcase only for my belongings. My questions were ignored by Abouna, for he did not know the answers, but he handed me a full dossier on the research I was supposed to be doing on ethnic groups of women in Urfa (Edessa) and Diyar Bakr (Amida) which consisted of the recording of memories of old women and visiting old quarters of the two towns where the women live. The programme was fictitious but the non-governmental organization was real. On taking leave, Abouna told me that the questions I put to him would be answered on the spot. He then told me after some hesitation that it came to their knowledge that the Turks knew about the mission due either to some leak on our part or to their very competent secret services in Palestine, and yet the Turks issued the visa, probably in the hope that my investigation would lead to the prophecy before the other and more powerful agents could put their hands on it, and thus it is expected they would be very cooperative and as such they will get the treasure without tears. Abouna finally said "remember, my child, that of all the agents seeking the treasure we are the weakest, with no government behind us, and yet, I have faith that the treasure promised to a Ghassanid will be found only by a Ghassanid. I will not say farewell, before we have our coffee". I realized, however, from the twitching of his lips that he wanted to talk. So he put his coffee cup down after making a noise in sipping it and said 'I am curious to know what made you say yes to this difficult mission and to assuming this burden". "Ah, Abouna" I said, "It is the longing for the unknown, the yearning for the unattainable, something that calls me outside of myself, a call a longing so persistent that for a moment I thought it could be assuaged by following the Sufi path, but my tranquility alas was ephemeral – an emptiness followed, a void that nothing could fill".

He was silent, pensive. "Yes, my child, I felt your longing for the infinite the first time I set my eyes upon you, but I had an inkling of all that before I met you, from the symbols which decorated your room".

"My room!" I said astonished" What has my room to do with all this. You have not seen my room as far as I know."

He laughed. "Sometimes your naivite's surprises me. I told you we had studied your past and present before the day we accosted you on the street. I learnt a great deal about you from the description Shimiram gave us of your room". "Shimiram" I cried "what has an Alawite maid from the Syrian mountains to do with you?"

He stroked his beard and laughed. "Shimiram is a Syriac from Jerusalem, whose family came from the same village in Turkey as mine, but ah, what a girl, a natural actress. We heard that your mother was replacing a maid who had gone blind, so we sent Shimiram to seek the job and to say she was an Alawite who years ago had come to seek work in Palestine. We knew that the world "Alawite" would arouse your historical curiosity and that you would persuade your mother to employ her. We even taught her the Alawite dialect and her job was to describe your house and its surroundings. The description of your room aroused my curiosity. She said it was bare, with a narrow iron bed like a monk's cell, but was full of pictures of cats and a dozen miniature sail boats. Your side table was full of silver hand mirrors. For me these three things where symbols that you chose subconsciously, compulsively, the sail boats indicated your longing for the unknown, the wide, wide sea, given that you were not born nor had lived by the sea, the mirrors could either be a desire to delve deep into yourself, to remove a veil behind the veil, to seek a meaning for your existence or could be narcissist egocentric shades. I could not tell which until I met you. This is not a reproach". He raised his hand. "No, do not interrupt, I know what you want to say, but I am not your judge" and he continued. 'As to the cats, a significant expression of your passion for another species – it lies behind your Sufi belief of the unity of all things". I jumped and gestured with my hands. "Abouna, you have catalogued me down to banalities. The reality is otherwise. I will debunk your hidden meaning behind the things in my room. The pictures on the walls are of my dead cat Simsim, my darling, my only love, my well beloved, whom I cannot replace. As to the sail boats, it is true I have never lived by the sea but it must be a vestige of another life – a past incarnation or an evocation of sailing towards the unknown. I concede that in this case your analysis is correct, as to the mirrors, they are of exquisite workmanship, isn't beauty enough, Abouna?

"You put me to shame, my child. I held many erroneous assumptions about you. You hid behind so many veils, you elude me. I lift one veil to find thousands beneath".

"May God give you a long life Abouna to prove or disprove your assumptions". You, my child have shed a light on my fading years and gave a meaning to my awakening before death which seems to have been prolonged. Remember you accused me of being like Sheherazade prolonging the tale night after night to save her life. You were right, my child, I was unconsciously doing the same with you, taking my time in telling you the story of the treasure little by little, to prolong this awakening before death – until you recuperate the treasure and I will verily set my eyes upon it". "But, Abouna", I said, "given that I find the treasure, it will take years for the scholars to decipher its contents. May your Gods, Huddud and Alluhu give you the time".

"Tut, tut. Do not blaspheme my child. I will only follow the law, for God causes the beginning, and ending of all things, conditions will be created that will enable me to receive that which accords with my being or that which is due to me, but dear Zuhra, I must now talk of practical things: you must have a smattering of Syriac, as you did of Turkish, to use in a Turkish souk. A teacher will come to your village while you prepare for the voyage to give you a few lessons. You will let it be known that you need that for your research with the international non-governmental organization. It is time to bid you farewell for I shall not see you before your journey, dear Zuhra. I wish for you to walk in gardens, walk amongst the green, find laughter and joy and remain in God's keeping". Abouna blessed me and for the first time I bent and kissed his withered hand and for the first time I saw tears in his eyes.

112

I left the monastery and went into the maze that Abouna had led me, for I was on the verge of entering another dimension where the impossible is possible, where the limits of logic and reason are very loose, where reality is a mirage, a chimera and where dreams are real. I was bewitched and kept murmuring 'open sesame' for I knew with a sure foreknowledge that to enter the world of the future you only have to utter 'open sesame'. I felt Abouna was following my thought whispering to me. "You have entered the magic world" but as Sheherazade told the king "Tomorrow I will continue the tale, for dawn has come. Tomorrow the tale of the treasure will be resumed".

Chapter VI
Espionage Oblige

The journey was uneventful. I took the plane to Antalya and from there to Urfa by car. Every step was arranged to perfection. Fatigued, and a little bored, I lay down on the bed in a modest hotel in Urfa, hoping to rearrange my thoughts in my new surroundings and almost fell asleep when I heard a gentle knock at the door. "Who is it" I cried and a voice answered in perfect English "I came to take your shoes, Madam". I rushed to the door. "Shoes, shoes" and then I remembered "come in, No.1" and a middle-aged man, who looked slightly oriental, entered, limping. He had his hands on his lips and said in a whisper, "madam, I have identified three agents in this hotel – all Arabic speaking, one from Iraq, the other a Kurd, also from Iraq who is CIA and a third from Syria".

He said this in a rush and then remembered to identify himself. "I am the shoes shiner stationed at the eastern corner of the lobby' and then he said aloud "May I take your shoes to shine?" I was at a loss. My shoes were still in the suitcase, so I took off the pair I was wearing. He then whispered. "I will bring them back after dinner with more news" and he closed the door and vanished.

I wondered at this impromptu incursion minutes after I entered the hotel. No.1 could have waited a little, but then I had taken an immediate dislike to him; the Syriacs, I thought, are amateurs in this business of intelligence.

There were few people in the large dining room opening onto a terrace with vines and shrubs but nobody paid any attention. Ah, I thought, it is my ordinary look that arouses no reaction in men. I remembered Abouna telling the messenger priest after he met me for the first time, "Praise Alluhu she looks very ordinary – not the *femme fatale*' type of woman" but Abouna was not aware that I had arrived and was standing by the door. The messenger priest looked sheepish and embarrassed for not warning Abouna of my presence. I smiled at the memory and consoled myself in the dining room that my ordinary look gives me protection. I loitered in the lobby before gaining my room and soon enough there was a knock at the door and a loud voice outside in a pure English accent saying "Your shoes, Madam, I hope you will be satisfied". When I opened the door he handed me my shoes with a folded paper in one of them and he made a sign with his hands that I should tear the paper and then quickly vanished.

Curious and excited, I took the paper which was a short report on the situation.

"The Chaldean prophecy" was not heard of after the destruction of the monastery of Mar Ephrem and the dispersion of its occupants, until then it was in the possession of an old monk who guarded it with his life. The Syriac community knew of the existence of the prophecy since it came to Urfa in the 6th century stolen from Hira, but it did not know that one part was in Jerusalem. Its contents were the subject of mystery and conjecture with widespread rumours that it indicated the secret place of Alexandre's treasure – a terra incognito which they aspired to discover one day. The last monk who possessed it lied in a hovel, in extreme poverty after ejection from the monastery, but was served by a loyal Kurdish woman who worked for many years in the monastery. On his death, the Kurdish woman disappeared to her native village with whatever was left of his belongings, presumably with the prophecy. It is not known whether the old woman had relatives who inherited her belongings. At present there is a feverish search for the prophecy purely on speculation. I have identified three agents in this hotel. I still have to identify the agents of France, Russia and Britain, who are probably posing as archaeologists, anthropologist and professors from Western universities and research institutes. The Syrian and Iraqi agents are concentrating on questioning old Arab residents of Urfa, the CIA Kurdish agent is travelling around to nearby villages, inhabited by Kurds, questioning them in their native language". I tore the report up and went to bed to dream of the old Kurdish servant who told me that I was on a false route; there was no such manuscript ever.

The next morning I had to present my-self officially at the department of Social Affairs to discuss with those responsible, the research project I was undertaking for an NGO, about ethnic women as a cover. I was taken after a long tedious wait to see the official who was a lady, past her youth, with vestiges of former beauty on her face. She kept the pretence about my project, although I presumed she knew what my real mission was. The Turkish intelligence knew they would have the last laugh and were waiting for the prophecy to be found to seize it officially for Turkish law prohibited antiques and national treasures to be skirted out of the country.

When I stood to take my leave she looked me up and down and then said with a smirk on her face "Your shoes are very well shined – ah! It must be the old man in your hotel". I was flabbergasted. She was playing with me. Why did she want me to know that she knew about No.1? I supposed she was enjoying teasing and annoying foreign agents running after a chimera.

I walked blindly out of the building, shocked and confused. The show is ending before it has begun. No.1 rushed at me and the Turkish lady laughed at me.

118

I walked until I came to the bazaar for the souk in any oriental town is my great delight. I immersed myself in the shopping crowd looking for antiques, knowing that most were false or rubbish. I was bargaining heatedly in Arabic for an old coffee pot, when a man in a shop across the street cried out at the top of his voice. "Spice from China, cheap, cheap." I stopped dead, dropped the coffee pot and went straight into the shop opposite. "May I see your spice, No.3?" "Marhaba[1], marhaba Jerusalem" for that was my code name. "Come, come inside the shop".

"I saw you coming down the street. I could tell it was you from the description they gave me. But you look struck by thunder. Why are you so crestfallen Jerusalem" he said as he pulled a chair forward and shouted for tea from the café on the opposite side of the street. 'I have just come from the Department of Social affairs". "I see the old hag frightened you. She loves to do that, but don't worry, she is harmless". I heaved a sigh of relief. "The lady is a Turk, but of remote Syriac origin. She sympathizes with us, relax Jerusalem, we can talk here. It is not like your hotel full of microphones. But tell me, what did the old hag say that upset you so much?" I hesitated for I was on shaky ground. "The Turkish lady knew about No.1 and I thought he was maybe working for the Turks". He stood up and laughed. "No, no, not No.1. He could not

---

1 Marhaba – welcome.

be double. The old lady knew about him because she gets the report of Turkish intelligence". "I must say I am relieved, all this is too intricate and I have been here for only one day". I drank my tea with cardamom, bought a cheap and chic cardigan and got up to leave when he held my hand and said, "Enjoy the rest of the afternoon. Tomorrow you will be going to one of the villages by autobus where you will start questioning the older inhabitants about the Kurdish servant, under the guise of your research. Walk out of the hotel at ten o'clock and follow a boy wearing a red parka, keep some steps behind him and do not talk to him in the bus. You will be met upon reaching the village". I see," and I shook my head, "so the search is in the village, without any indication whatsoever". "We are visiting the villages because the other agents are doing so. It is leading us nowhere, but we may get a break. Goodbye for now. We will meet again" he said as he waved me goodbye.

For several days I visited villages surrounding Urfa. The list was long prepared by No.1 but I did not have one indication or one lead that could throw light on the family of the Kurdish servant.

One morning I refused to go to the villages and went instead to the square around the mosque where our agent No. 4 was stationed, selling old books and manuscripts. I did not identify myself and he did not recognize me. It was a pleasure talking to him of old books and things, for he was a former professor of history.

My plea to No.1 to cut my visits to the countryside was met negatively but when I insisted he said that we would search Urfa after we had finished our round of the villages. I told him I was sick and tired of disturbing and annoying the poor peasants asking them if they had anything old for sale.

I went to the dining room in a very bad mood when I noticed that only two tables were occupied, each by a solitary man, both looked Arab but I fought against the impulse of talking to them for I was getting tired of seeing only Turks and Kurds. A third man came in and sat at the table next to mine. He immediately snapped his fingers for the waiter and started to order in a boisterous and vulgar voice dishes that were not on the menu. The waiter informed him politely at first that he could only order what was there on the menu. The man began to shout abuse at the waiter and at the owners of the hotel. I looked sideways to see one of the Arabs get up from his table and walk to the waiter saying loudly in Arabic. "Don't let that lousy Kurd intimidate you. If the food is not good enough let him go elsewhere for he is bursting with CIA dollars". So that is the Kurdish agent. Surely the Americans could have picked somebody less vulgar, I said to myself.

121

Meanwhile, the Kurd rose from the table shaking his fist, ready to hit the Arab, shouting in guttural Arabic. "I know who you are, a Ba'athist dog in disguise, pretending to be working for the new Iraqi government". The other Arab rose to join the melee shouting. "You dare speak of the Ba'ath when you are a Kurdish pig in the service of the Americans". The Kurd was foaming. "Iraqi spy, Syrian spy, former Ba'athist pimps." Before he finished he was hit in his bulging stomach by the Iraqi and fell on the floor while the waiter dragged him out of the room, cursing obscenely. "You will pay for this".

The two Arabs looked at each other and laughed while I asked them to join me. "Hala, hala – from your accent you are from Palestine" the Syrian said. We all shook hands. "So you are the lady in this show they told me about, but let us have something to eat before that dog sends us the Turkish police" and he crossed his hands "to put us in chains'. "Don't worry" said the Iraqi. "There is no love lost between the Turkish police and a CIA Kurd".

We talked and talked of everything, except our respective missions. I told them that I was touched by how the Syrian stood up for the Iraqi. "Sister" they both said. "We are Arabs and Ba'athist Arabs at that, but in disguise" and they both laughed.

The police escorted by the manager came in before we finished our meal. "The lady is not involved" said the waiter to the policeman. "She happened to be dining during the incident". I got up and excused myself when the police asked me "you witnessed it all?" "Yes", I said "the Kurd insulted the waiter in an unacceptable revolting way" and walked up to my room.

In my room I chuckled. I have met three agents all at once and was amazed by the way the two Arabs were careless about their mission. I still have to meet three more spies, French, British and Russian, but who knows, I may have already met them.

I did not know until the next morning when the waiter informed me that the Iraqi and Syrian were taken to the police station and probably spent their night in jail. Their rooms were empty but he confided in a whisper that the police must have done that as a gesture to satisfy the Americans for they make a big fuss when any of their citizens is concerned and more so since the Kurd is their agent, and for a small incident like that of yesterday they go so far as to protest to the Minister of the Interior in Ankara. The two Arabs walked sheepishly in, just as I was finishing breakfast and coming to my table they said they had a hilarious night in the Turkish jail, for the police were especially nice to them although they neither love the Syrians nor Iraqis but it is the Kurds they hate most and they would have liked to jail the vicious Kurd instead of them. The waiter came in smiling to join our circle saying that the Kurd had taken his baggage and left early in the morning. The incident in itself revealed the tensions in the region between the Arabs and the Kurds who affiliated themselves with the Americans in Iraq.

The next day I informed No.1 in passing the shoeshine corner in the lobby that I was going to buy some books in the square near the mosque where I would meet again with No.4. I went out in the faint Autumn sunshine and stopped for a cup of coffee in the courtyard of an old khan with pots of fragrant herbs and flowers all around. I felt in harmony with my surroundings, with the world as a whole and forgot my impossible mission and the chimera I was seeking. But it all came back as I walked towards the mosque – a woman amongst five men – what an astonishing choice of the Committee of Nine, their mistaken belief that the woman is more discreet, delicate, subtle and that she could outwit the men. True the agents I already met were not brilliant by any means and neither careful nor prudent, but what about the other occidental three? I was happy in the corner of the square with the piles of ancient books in Arabic, Turkish, Armenian and Syriac and started handling them when I saw the owner, the history teacher whom I already met, sitting on a straw mat against the wall of the mosque eyeing me intensely. I left the books and walked towards him when he asked me in Arabic "you came before and bought nothing, what books are you seeking, young woman". "I am seeking old manuscripts No.4".

124

He put his hand forward and I bent to shake it. "I cannot get up easily, Jerusalem. I have a backache". "How is it you speak Arabic so well no.4?" He laughed "because I am an Arab, Jerusalem – you know that Urfa in the recent past had a large Arabic and Syriac population. All gone, massacred, exiled, but there are a few fossils like me left". I love your dialect with its hard "K". "It is the Mosul dialect" I said, delighted "ah, that is the dialect of all southern Turkey, which was once part of Syria. He then clapped his hands for a lad who was standing nearby. "You will have tea or coffee?" he asked. "Tea please," he then asked the lad to bring a stool for me and ordered tea from the coffee house nearby.

I moved the stool and sat near to him but he pointed to his right ear. "I am deaf on this side, please move your stool to the left" he said. We talked of old things as we did when we first met, of the town, of the weather and only after we drank our tea in the miniature cups he turned to me and said "Listen carefully, Jerusalem. There is a man who comes here every day and looks at the books without buying any and without talking to me. I think he is a western agent but from his looks he could be French, English or maybe Russian. He will come soon. Try to talk to him, another thing I understand you are going daily to the surrounding villages to look for the heirs of the Kurdish servant but, according to me it is all in vain. I have strong reasons to believe that the Kurdish servant

125

died here in Urfa. It is here in this town that you must seek the Kurdish heirs. I have few indications that I will give you. Ah, here, I see the man coming. Walk about and try to meet him". At these words I quickly got up and started handling the pile of books at my side but the man did not come near. I saw him going to the other book seller a little further on the square. I followed discreetly and concentrated on handling a pile of Arabic books when I heard a voice in Arabic. "May I help you?" I turned around to look into translucent pale blue eyes in a tanned oval face that had the perfection of a classical icon oh lord! I said to myself, he is beautiful. I opened my mouth to say thank you but all I said was "do you speak Arabic?" He smiled and replied "yes, I do. You are an Arab I presume". "Yes", I said. "And you?" I asked. 'Can you guess?" "You must be either English, French, or perhaps Russian.

He laughed. "I see you are very subtle as I am neither English nor French. Must be Russian mustn't I?" In his voice there was mockery and in his eyes there was doubt. I was silent for it was obvious he was the Russian agent and that he spotted me as I spotted him. "Boris Borisov, engineer, former professor of oriental languages at the Moscow Language Institute" he said as he inclined his head. I gave him my name and said I was a sociologist. I remembered that his institute was mainly for diplomats as a cover for intelligence agents but he was in Urfa as an engineer.

126

He broke the silence by saying "We always stood for the Palestinians you know". "That was in the past" I corrected him. "The Soviets did". "Ah, ah! we Russians do not deny our past". We walked around and talked of books, of Moscow that I have visited three times and we parted after I accepted his invitation to dinner the following night in his hotel, which was a grade higher than mine. When he left I stood saying to myself 'Alas, Abouna's warning not to fall in love is of no use, I knew the signs. I was falling in love with that harmonious perfection of a face; the way he walked, his Arabic with no foreign resonance, oh Allah! what shall I do? I went in circles in my mind. Why did he tell me that I was Palestinian, thus revealing that he knew all about me? In reality he was seeking my complicity by reminding me that the Russians were always on the side of the Palestinians. My complicity perhaps would lead him to the treasure and for such a high hope he deliberately put on all his charm.

I went back to the hotel without stopping to speak to No.4. He would see it all on my face. But I was alive; I looked at the few dresses I had brought with me to find one fit for a dinner with him. I was sorry I had very little make-up with me for my feminine vanity was aroused. Ah this exhileration and vibration of being that only love can give, steady, steady old girl, but after all, this is only the beginning. The best part of an avalanche of a coming love, but then, this sudden feeling must mean that it is filling a void, of loneliness in a strange land. A knock on the door pulled me out of this turmoil and I opened the door, expecting No.1. It was a maid who serves the second floor. "Madam" she said. I have come to take your lingerie for washing and ironing". "Come in No.2" I said for until now, No.2 had not shown any sign. As I handed her some underwear she put a folded paper in my hand and disappeared. I unfolded the paper but could not read the message – the words were illegible but with the help of a magnifying glass I read in French *"mèfiez-vous de l'agent Russe"*. I wanted to take my bag and run. Run where? – to a car to take me to the airport at Antalya? Crestfallen, I went to dinner to see the two Arabs sitting sullen at seperate tables, as discouraged as I was, to judge from their faces. The next day, waiting for dinner time seemed so very long but in the evening I was meticulously dressed, brushing my hair for the tenth time when the call came from the doorman that a gentleman was waiting for me in the lobby. I went down with a face I hoped it would not show a trace of emotion.

He was standing there in all his radiant beauty and I could not help but tell him that he must be of ancient Greek descent. "You are right" he said smiling. "How did you know?" "Just like you knew I was Palestinian" I retorted "but seriously, I must have inherited a trace of the science of genealogy for it was well known among the ancient Arabs". "You know there were many Byzantine families who settled in

128

Russia after the fall of Constantinople. My mothers' family claims to be one of them". We walked through the lobby when I saw the Iraqi Arab smirking behind me and saying loudly "Good evening, my sister". I turned around saying "Meet my Russian friend who speaks Arabic". "We have met before" said the Russian. "Ah yes, many times in the countryside".

A car was waiting to take us to his hotel. "What luxury" I said and resigned myself to an evening where the Russian is going to pick my brains but to the contrary we talked of Moscow, of Jerusalem, of Russian icons and orthodoxy. Both of us were born Orthodox. I was struck by his intelligence his 'savoir faire', his delicate attention and fell deeper and deeper in his snare. He was natural and elegant. A rare bird, needless to say, we set another date. I invited him to dinner but he refused, insisting that the invitation be his. When I said goodnight to him at the door of my hotel I thought how could I bear to be away from him and I went to my room in a daze, remembering the words of Confucius. "Things that accord together in tone vibrate together. Things that have affinity in their innermost natures seek one another". Boris and I were on the same level of vibration. What is happening is inevitable but neither the Russian intelligence, ex KGB, nor the committee of nine ever envisaged that.

I knew I was being watched by our four agents from shoes to books besides all the others. I was walking on air. I did not mind their nasty looks or their sniggers and although my days were spent in the villages, the evenings were mine with him. I was happy, but besides my happiness lurked the fear that he would open the subject of the manuscript and he would ask me to collaborate with him to find it. But he never did. We were just two people in love.

One evening, just as we finished dinner, a handsome, well-dressed man came into the dining room. He smiled at Boris and walked to our table. Boris introduced him as an archaeologist with the French CNRS, working in a dig near the ancient city of Amida (Diyar Bakr).I surmised that he was staying in the hotel and we asked him to join us. I pestered him with questions about the dig and he gallantly invited me to visit the site. When he left to have his dinner, Boris whispered teasingly. "Now you have met all the spies". My heart missed a beat, for this was the second time Boris alluded to our quest. "What a happy family we make" he said in the same bantering tone. "No, no", I said. "I have not met the Brit". On hearing me say that Boris laughed in a grotesque way. "Don't say you haven't met him – you already have'. I was stunned. "How, where, who is he?" I asked, but he laughed softly this time and said cryptically with a note of pity in his voice. "My poor dear, you are in for a great surprise".

A long silence followed. "It is stuffy in here. We need some air", Boris said as he got up, ignoring my presence and walked ahead of me to the door. I followed him, but something in my heart broke. How could I fall so badly for a rival agent, who may be using me for his own ends. I then remembered Abouna's warning about falling in love, and it became clear in my besotted mind that I meant nothing to Boris. I was only a tool and my blood boiled at the idea of being used. What did I expect from Boris? That he would tell me all because he was in love? No, no, it was a fake love and I started to tremble but then he took my arm and whispered tender words and the enchantment returned.

The next day things fell into focus for I already met five agents looking for the manuscript, the Iraqi, Syrian, American, French and Russian, and according to Boris I had already met the British agent. I searched my mind – who could it be amongst all the people I had met? I could not pin my suspicion on anyone. They all had official covers for being in Urfa, the Russian was an engineer deployed by his government to help build a dam, the Frenchman was discovering ruins, the Iraqi was a commercial attaché at the Embassy in Ankara, supposedly buying dried fruits for Baghdad, the Syrian was a teacher of Arabic and I was doing sociological and ethnic research. I wondered what the Briton was doing and under what disguise. I also resolved not to ask Boris for any information for I saw how his whole comportment changed when I asked him about the Briton. I must have fallen in love with a Dr. Jeckel and Mr. Hyde type but isn't that what all spies or agents are supposed to be?

I visited my favourite haunt, the book corner by the mosque and had tea with No.4 who shook his head and told me frankly. I "warned them that this job was not for a young woman, especially an over-sensitive one, who can fall easily in love. "I ignored his crudeness and said 'it was you who asked me to meet him and talk to him remember'. He shook his head. "I did, indeed I did, but I did not foresee". "What did you not foresee?" "Please sit down and calm yourself. I gave an advice that you did not follow, it is in the poorest quarter of this town that you should conduct your search". And then he added as an afterthought, "the other agents are also searching in the villages, ha, ha, ha, what fools". "You forget" I replied, "that it is No.1 who arranged my programme and the places I visit". "Alluhu, Alluhu', he cried 'an independent woman like you can make her choice and decide on her own programme, for after all we are only here to help you, not to dictate to you". I was grateful, for his words were balm to my troubled and confused vision of things. The next morning when No.1 handed me my old pair of shoes which he shined every day, a note indicating my targets for the day, I told him that I would spend my day in town and when he started to protest I told him that I would arrange my programme as I see fit and that was that and closed my door.

I went to the main souk and from there took a taxi to the most sordid part of the town which No.4 indicated and I walked leisurely between the hovels and the open-sided sheds. I felt free, without constraint, for no one I believed followed me here. I wondered where Boris was conducting his search. We never met during the day nor talked about our respective visits, but the evenings were ours and the thought of another night with him filled me with joy. I was besotted and yet I knew that his situation is ephemeral – *carpe diem* – I could not envisage a lifetime with him where husband and wife are always nagging and carping at each other. Deep in my thought I came upon a coffee house in a crumbling shed, with stools around little tables where a few men were enjoying the shisheh (nargila). I went in and sat on a stool in the corner to the surprise of the owner, seeing what he took to be a foreign tourist in his humble shed, far from the places foreigners frequent. He gestured with his hands, thinking I do not understand his language, but when I said I wanted some coffee in the little Turkish I had learned, he ran happily shouting "Coffee, coffee to the Khatun".

He came back all smiles, with a round brass tray with a coffee pot, a small cup and a glass of water. I opened my bag to pay him when I noticed a dirty torn carpet underneath my feet. I stared at it as he followed my look. "Old, old, carpet" as he pointed to the holes in it. But it was an ancient Ghiordes prayer rug with

133

patches of a rare green colour, the best that Turkey produced. I wanted it so badly and asked him if I could buy it and started to produce some coins from my bag. He was indignant and sad with hurt pride. "Khatun, my name is Balend. I may be poor but I do not sell my old carpet. "Please tell me Balend from where did you buy it?" I said meekly. Bored by the whole affair, Balend said: "It was given to me by Haji Yunis from his rubbish heap". "But where is this rubbish dump. Can I go there?" I asked. Balend reflected, scratched his head and turned around to the few people sitting in the back of the shed and said in Turkish, which I understood. "Listen to that – she wants to go to the Khan". "No, no", they shouted. "Tell her it is inhabited by the jinn". He then turned to me. "Khatun, the Kahn of Haji Yunis was closed by the municipality three years ago". He obviously did not want to tell me about the jinn but I was obstinate, my mad obsession with flea markets and *marchès aux puces* took over. Please ask Haji Yunis to open the khan for me" I pleaded. "but Khatun, what do you want with rubbish?" I want to buy an old carpet like yours" I said. The few men in the shed shook their heads in disbelief and started talking so quickly I could neither follow nor understand but I saw that Balend was enjoying himself. "Listen", he said to the audience, "she wants to buy a carpet from the khan, if she only knew." They laughed, but were ashamed, for Turks are very polite to foreigners. One of the men spoke to me. "Khatun, Turkey makes beautiful carpets, if you want to buy one, but not from the Khan". "But I like old and torn carpets" I insisted. "Please ask Haji Yunis to take me to his khan". They looked at each other as if to say, she is a little mad like all these foreigners who come to turkey and one of them said in a loud whisper, "poor lady, who is going to tell her about the jinn?"

I left the shed, wretched but very curious about the jinn, but not before I brazenly bribed Balend by giving him an amount of money that made his eyes pop and only said "would you please find Haji Yunis and tell him that I want to visit his khan".

I left the sordid part of the town and headed straight to the souk, where on my approach I heard No.3 shouting to sell jewellery instead of spice. He welcomed me into the shop and showed me his jewellery in front of the other customers. When they left he said a little embarrassed 'I have a message for you. It came to our knowledge that you are following your own programme". I interrupted him for I knew what was coming. "Listen, No.3" I said, "tell your network that I will follow any schedule I choose. It is I who decide and if they try to hinder or annoy me I will leave the whole mess and return, let them find the "prophecy". He was aghast. All he could say was "Madam, your tea". I noticed that he did not use my code name. "I do not want any tea thank you" and left the shop without giving him a glance.

My life took a new pattern, for after this episode no one came my way again. The only one of the network with whom I kept in contact was No.4, the books. I spent my mornings in the old town, my afternoons loitering around the mosque and in the souk and my evening with Boris. I returned to the coffee shed without much success and Balend would only say "Haram, Haram". Never, never go to the Khan, but gradually I wore his resistance by the amount of money I kept increasing every time, until one morning he greeted me with a large smile. I make you happy today. Yes, Yes". And after waiting to see my reaction he said 'Haji Yunis is waiting for you" and a well-dressed young man who was out of place in this shoddy and squalid place, rose from the back corner, saying in the traditional Turkish way, "Marhaba, a thousand Marhaba Khatun". I replied with a long and effusive greeting before he asked me why on earth I wanted to go to the khan. "to buy a carpet" I said. "true, there are heaps of old carpets, but didn't Balend tell you that it is inhabited by the jinn?". I laughed. "The jinn do not frighten me for I come from the Holy City of Jerusalem". "On your head be it" he said sternly and walked beside me to the derelict old khan that once had seen better days but now was falling apart. Yunis told me that his aging father bought it many years ago when it was abandoned and spent a lifetime collecting the belongings of deceased persons who had no families and the rubbish that the municipality could not collect, especially from old

136

abandoned buildings. He sometimes fell on priceless pieces, silver, carpets and even jewellery which he sold to antique shops for tourists and thus made a fortune". "What about you?" I asked. "Me, I never touched the place – full of cockroaches and rats. "But I thought it was inhabited by the jinn". "It is the abode of the jinn of Urfa, but the jinn seem to cohabit very well with the rats".

When he opened the squeaking door I nearly chocked, for a cloud of dust and the batting of wings met us. "It is the bats, I warn you, it is full of rats and serpents. I won't go in with you. I will sit outside while you have a look. You will find that the rats have eaten the carpets". He put his hand to cover this nose, for the smell of decay was overwhelming. "I will leave you with the rats and the jinn. I will wait outside in the pallid sun to smoke my pipe".

Left alone I was overjoyed when I saw the heaps of carpets, saddlebags, old Turkish robes and broken furniture. I found a bamboo stick and started poking into the heaps, the first thing I pulled was a carpet saddlebag with a beautiful design but riddeled with holes and caked with dirt, but before I poked into the next heap my heart stopped for an inhuman cry of pain rang in the hall. I was petrified with fear. It was like an animal having its throat cut but luckily Haji Yunis' shadow framed the door. He was shaking. 'I warned you, you are disturbing the jinn with this incursion into their habitat". I did not answer but my eyes were searching the small niches in the wall trying to locate the source of the voice. "Haji Yunis refused to put his foot inside the door. "Come, Khatun, we have to go".

On the way out his tongue loosened up "The khan was condemned by the Baladiya (municipality) after the inhabitants of the quarter complained. What you heard today is only a foretaste of the horror the khan holds. Closing the khan almost ruined my father financially but the authorities paid him a large compensation. In its heyday this khan was a gold mine for its owners, but then it began to lose its clientele because people began to disappear mysteriously. A caravan would lose one or two merchants during the night, presumably assassinated and their rich merchandise vanished like them into thin air, before the authorities could put their hands on the culprits. The khan acquired a horrible reputation and was abandoned for many years until my father bought it. The cry you heard today is a warning and I cannot take the responsibility of your meeting with an accident inside". I was so upset I could hardly speak. "Please", I pleaded with him. "I saw some beautiful carpets – let me come again. I will write a note that I entered the khan on my own responsibility". Yunis realized that I was shaken so we stopped at a coffee house in the neighbourhood and he continued his tale of the khan. "Listen to me Khatun, It is said that the last man killed inside before it was closed, was a young nobleman from Baghdad, on his way to Istanbul to meet his

138

bride. He stopped to spend the night in Urfa with his retinue and saddle bags filled with silks and exquisite jewelry for his bride, while news of his forthcoming arrival reached Istanbul, where the bride was made ready with henna and the bridal gown while the dancing girls and tambourines assembled on the terrace of the palace to greet the bridegroom who never came. The gifts he was carrying were missing but the strangest thing is that his retinue denied hearing anything during the night. It is rumoured that the animal cry we heard today was his, while they were cutting his throat".

"Haji Yunis" I said "are you telling me this to warn me: I am not that easily frightened". That was pure bravado on my part for I was shaken and troubled. "You are a strange one Khatun, pretending you are not afraid. I admit I am. I only accepted to take you to the khan, thus breaching the law out of curiosity to see what kind of a foreign woman you are for Balend did not tell me you were Arab. I have Arab ancestry myself and I think you must have a reason to insist on going again". "Yes, Haji Yunis, I do. I am looking not only for old carpets but old books and manuscripts that may be in the rubbish". "Ah, my father said he collected plenty of that".

We walked silently to my hotel where I put a larger sum of dollars in his pocket. He made the gesture of refusal but then relented and said "I will wait for you at Balend, tomorrow morning. Maybe by Allah's grace you could find your books".

Boris noticed my disarray and tried to lighten my spirit by taking me to a little restaurant in town where we had one sort of kebab and dolmas[1] to my heart's content. I noticed that Boris was always on the verge of asking me a question but he did not, the only remark he made was that I had not been seen lately in the villages and to that I gave no answer and did not mention my visit to the khan.

In my bed I had nightmares hearing that shriek again so I sat upright with all the lights on so I would not fall asleep, what was I doing in this strange land? What have I to do with ancient Chaldeans and modern Syriacs? The idea of the Ghassanids irritated me more for what link have I with Al-Harith bin Jabla who never heard or dreamed of such a treasure and of his soldier the Archangel Gabriel? I cried with pathos for all things but above all for Boris, who is seeking a treasure in vain, for a love that had to end before its fulfillment, for having to close my heart against longing for him, for parting, for fate. It was already morning as I was aroused from this whirlpool of emotion by soft taps on the door. It was No.1 who asked me if I were ill, when he saw my puffed red eyes and swollen face. I told him I was tired and needed to rest. He seemed embarrassed and after shifting his feet

---

1 Dolma – Stuffed vine leaves.

he said stammering, "If you will excuse me I have to tell you it is not wise to see the Russian agent so often. You know as well as I do that he is trying to pick your brain, to exploit you". I laughed in his face. "What if it is the other way round No.1,. Would you then approve? And now, if you will excuse me I have to bathe and dress; I do have a full day ahead and a rendez-vous with the Russian agent."

At dinner with Boris I played the comedy by bantering him for his solemn mood but he saw through me and said "Zuhra, why are you so sad?" I answered by bursting into tears.

At night on my narrow bed in a sordid room in an anonymous hotel the mood persisted as I thought of the Ghassanids and the sadness of my whole race. I was drugged into sleep where I dreamed that I was an old crone lying paralysed in my sick bed when an old Haji, father of Yunis came stealthily to my hut and started collecting my belongings. I began to shout, 'I am not dead, get out you thief". The Haji barred his teeth like a mad dog and said "Quiet, you witch, I am collecting on the order of the Baladiya" and he went pulling my bundles and saddlebags from under the bed. I woke up shaken for the saddle bag of the dream rang a bell as I had seen it in the rubbish heap. This I said to myself is an indication: I must get that saddle bag out of the khan. I dressed hurriedly and walked out of the hotel without breakfast to the shed where I found Haji Yunis waiting for me, looking at his watch and groaning because I was late. I forced a smile and refused to leave the shed without coffee, while he was shaking his head and saying "no more of this, it is the last time". I said nothing and walked beside him and then he said out of the blues. "This nonsense you told me yesterday about your seeking manuscripts and books, is only a cover. For if you are expecting to find the treasure of the bridegroom you are sadly mistaken for the khan was turned upside down by my father and by the Baladiya. Every heap of rubbish was combed and nothing was ever found". In the khan I pulled two carpets that I liked from one of the piles and put them aside. Haji Yunis stood at the door and clapped his hands. "Yallah" he said. On parting I handed him more dollars and said 'only one more time and I will give up". He grunted, counted the dollars and agreed. I murmured thanks to the Committee of Nine whose generosity enabled me to buy the good grace of Haji Yunis.

In the evening Boris asked me what I had seen that had made me so happy. "A piece of rubbish" I said laughing. "Does that surprise you?" "No, nothing you do surprises me, for you are a heap of contradiction. "Better than a heap of rubbish" I said mockingly, but Boris saw through me. He felt I was onto something for by now he felt frustrated. His search was at a standstill and the Institute in Moscow must have been nagging him and for the first time since I met him, he expressed a certain pessimism and a certain affection.

142

"I am a little homesick for Moscow" and when I looked at him he said "you make life here bearable". And that was the first and last compliment he ever gave me! I was full of expectation and excitement when I met Haji Yunis at the door of the khan the next day at noon. I had a presentiment as if a magnet, an unseen force was pulling me to the farthest corner of the hall, where the heap of carpets and saddlebags lay. I poked the heap with my bamboo stick violently which aroused a cloud of dust that almost choked me and made me cough so loudly that Yunis stood at the door and shouted "Yallah, Yallah, come out, this place will kill you". I signaled with my hand for him to go away and resumed my poking, pulling several saddlebags on the side, one of them bulged: it had something inside. I bent down and fuddled with its leather straps which crumbled at my touch and lo, I pulled a parchment wrapped in cloth that like the leather straps, crumbled into dust into my hands. My heart stood still. I found the manuscript. I looked at the Syriac writing that enveloped the parchment and with the little Syriac that I acquired in Jerusalem I read with difficulty the name of the 6th century bishop who stole the prophecy!

There are moments one cannot describe, like when I held the prophecy in my hands. I felt humbled, for it was not ability on my part that I had found it. Benevolent unseen forces had led me. I quickly wrapped the manuscript in one of the carpets and called Haji Yunis that I had had enough and needed a hammal (porter) to carry my two carpets to the hotel, but Haji Yunis told me that I was crazy to think we would find one in this poor area, so he carried the carpets to the shed where Balend volunteered to go and buy a suitcase and to find a hammal and came back with both. Shoved my treasure into the suitcase and thanked both Haji Yunis and Balend for their help before I said goodbye. Haji Yunis looked at me enquiringly saying "the Khatun must have found what she sought. Could she be so happy about two dirty smelly torn carpets? Only Allah knows what she has found".

I asked the hammal to follow me to the mosque and stopped at the corner of No.4. "I came to buy the Arabic books I saw the other time" I told him and I bought enough books to cover the carpets in the suitcase and held two in my hand. I was covering myself for the news of the suitcase full of books would be going around amongst the network of spies.

In the hotel lobby I came across No.1 who tried to take my suitcase from the hammal. I thanked him and said I needed the hammal to take it up because I had to give him some money. I was amazed at the servility of No.1 for he had shunned me since I refused to follow his programme.

In my room I locked the door behind me and pulled the prophecy from the carpets under the books. I scraped the dirt and the dust and wrapped it in one of my nightgowns. I handled it with reverence and tenderness like that of a lover and put it in the chest of drawers with my lingerie. I then sat on the bed and wept, for the release of tension over the last weeks, for the unseen forces that had led me to the treasure. I wept for the faithful Kurdish servant who kept the treasure of her master in a saddlebag under her bed and whose belongings ended in the poor man's khan abode of the jinn. In my excitement and jubilation I needed to see Boris from whom I must keep my secret.

I do not wish it on anybody, be it friend or foe, to pass the evening as I did, knowing that my time with him was at an end. He was totally ignorant of this destiny.

Boris suddenly asked. "How is your lame shoe shiner?" He is neither lame nor a shoe-shiner, nor of Iranian origin as he claims" I said. "His English is curious he slips from cockney to a perfect upper class accent". "Tra la la" said Boris, "so you begin to see". His words lifted the scales from my eyes and removed that veil that clouded my mind. I realized too late that No.1 was the British agent that I had not met. I never was so shocked and I said feebly, "but he is our No.1". Boris laughed, "double my dear, he missed being a tripple agent for he offered to work for us too!".

No.1 was a double agent and I was cheating the man I loved, for a while he was furtively knocking his

145

head, searching for the treasure I had hidden in my chest of drawers. 'I am at a loss, Boris, between truth and falsehood". Boris was on the alert. "What makes you say that?" I ignored his question, for me there was one truth, one loyalty, I was a Ghassanid, a symbolic owner of the treasure and that had to come before love. I wondered why he had to warn me against no.1, was it out of consideration for me or a sort of vengeance against the British agent. I thanked my stars that I did not follow the instructions I was given according to which, in case I found the treasure, No.1 was to make all the arrangements to whisk the prophecy out of the country under the nose of the Turks, luckily Boris warned me in time, for No.1 would have arranged to hand it to the British on the way and find an excuse for its loss.

I decided to seek help from No.4 who inspired me with confidence, so I went to see him and asked him to contact Jerusalem. No.4 jumped for joy. "What! You really found it". I put my fingers to my lips. "Please, repeat to them the password *'open sesame'* and they will give instructions for the next step. "Not so fast, young lady, this is a job for No.1. I cannot supersede him". "Yes, yes, you can. I am the rightful owner of the treasure, responsible for recuperating it and I ask you to do this job. You can if you prefer inform them in Jerusalem that No.1 is a double agent". He was shocked into silence. "Come back in two days. The arrangements will be made".

146

I took a taxi to meet Boris in the small Turkish restaurant in the old city where we usually ate dolma, fried aubergine and kefta (meat balls). I heard his honeyed voice exercising his Turkish with the waiter before I entered. Oh what joy and then I stopped. it was my last night with him but he does not know it. And it suddenly dawned upon me that the thrill of finding the treasure meant parting with the beloved, the end of this brief period of time with its exquisite joy of being with Boris! I was torn and broken, but then I remembered I was a Ghassanid given a treasure that was due to my ancestor Harith and his soldier, the Archangel Gabriel. I straightened my shoulders and felt proud that no love can interfere with my Ghassanid loyalty. The minute Boris saw me he said "you were crying, come now, tell old Boris what happened". I wish I could tell him I thought, but aloud I said "just a little homesickness".

On the appointed day the book seller explained the plan of my flight from Urfa in detail. I must bring him my clothes in small bundles so as not to attract attention, after which I was to simulate illness of the liver and he indicated the symptoms I would be suffering from. My ticket to Jerusalem will be bought in Antalya. I agreed with the plan except for handing him the manuscript. I told him "I will keep it with me at all times and under all circumstances and with that I left him, sullen and unhappy. When I walked away he called me back to tell me "until then follow your normal routine and now if you will excuse me some clients are waiting and so I was dismissed.

Two days in which I will follow my usual round of visiting the old town, indulging in my favourite exercise, bargaining in the souk for old trinkets, cornelian seals and fake emerald rings, waiting for the evening with Boris, for I decided on another evening, in which I could not hide the flow of my love and saw hardly any glimpse of his, the doubt gnawing my heart grew that his love was only a simulation. On my last night, I sent him a word that I was ill, because I could not go through the torture of another evening, another parting. I wrote that I would see him for dinner the next evening, a promise which I had no intention of keeping.'

The next morning I remained in bed, rang for my breakfast and complained of an atrocious pain. The pain grew more fierce the next day, and my groans were heard in the corridor of the hotel. No.1, who missed nothing, came to see me and looked at me with distaste which made me groan louder in his presence. The hotel manager came up and said he would send me a doctor. All was going as planned by No. 4.

My so-called sick nights where full of nightmares again and again I dreamed I was the Kurdish hag, lying on a dirty bed with atrocious pains, cold and hungry, crying for help from my master, the monk of Mar Ephrem. I saw the door open and a

148

dignified man came in and instead of looking at me he was pulling my bundles from under my bed. "I collect the rubbish of dead people" he said "I am not dead, not dead" but he paid no heed. He gathered the pots and pans and pulled the saddlebag that my master made me promise to keep. "May Allah punish you in the fires of hell" I cried. I woke up, trembling. This repeated nightmare was the malediction of the old hag. It first struck Haji Yunis, for shortly afterwards his Khan was closed and he lost his livelihood and now she comes to me in dreams. I called upon the mercy of Allah and when night came I asked the reception for a candle and incense. I burned the incense on a plate, lit the candle and prayed for the repose of the old woman's soul and fell into a sleep without dreams.

My sham sickness increased with boredom so the hotel manager came up to my room with a well-known Turkish doctor from Istanbul who was on a visit to his home town Urfa, he was also a childhood friend of the bookseller No.4 who must have briefed him on the whole affair. He gave me three kinds of medicine which we both knew I would not take and left my room, looking worried and shaking his head, telling the manager that I had to be transferred to the hospital. I protested and pretended a loathing of hospitals but the doctor insisted. I was told to make ready for the ambulance that would come at dusk and instead of being jubilant to leave I was sad that I did not see or hear from Boris during my illness. He had surely heard that I was ill, but, "espionage oblige!"

The ambulance came, with me wrapped in two blankets, under which was the prophecy. No.1 was at the door to see me off and I only nodded, without saying goodbye.

In the ambulance I found my suitcase and my books and false nurses. The ambulance stopped in front of a house near the hospital where No.4 was waiting. I changed my clothes, took leave of the fake nurses and rode beside No.4 in his station wagon all the way to Antalya airport. In the airport No.4 escorted me to the plane for fear of a Turkish search for artefacts forbidden to leave the country, but the prophecy was secure under my light coat. I thanked him and he said goodbye with such relief for he whispered to me that he was afraid I would be kidnapped by one of the agents if they became aware of my flight from Urfa. Only when the plane taxied out of Antalya did I realize how frightened I was and when relaxation came I began to wonder at the effect of this clandestine flight. The Turks and the other agents who were no fools would blindly go on searching the outskirts of Urfa until their respective intelligence services found out that the prophecy was already safe in Jerusalem. I thought about the loss of face the Syrian and Iraqi agents would be met with when they returned empty handed. As for the British who put their faith in a double agent, either from ignorance which I doubt, or from a diabolical plan to take it smoothly, easily from the Syriac agent, that is poor me if I found it – their plans would have worked to perfection because I would have handed it to No. 1, had Boris not warned me.

As to the French who always care for form rather than substance, their agent would console them by discovering a Greek temple or a statue in Amida, but Boris, it is too painful to think of what he would face in Moscow and what he would think of my cheating him. One day if we ever meet again I must explain to him that I could not deviate from a promise given to a man on his deathbed one thousand five hundred years ago and I, a genetically proven Ghassanid, had to respect the vow and the promise. I laughed inwardly with great pleasure when I saw in my mind's eye No.1 hopping mad on his false lame foot lamenting the loss of his prey as to the Kurdish CIA. I hope he will receive the punishment he deserves. The Turks who were waiting for the prophecy to be found by one of the agents when they would coldly appropriate it without tears would now expel all the spies from the country as *persona non grata*.

Chapter VII

Introduction to the report

In Jerusalem I went straight to the monastery to hand over the manuscript. Abouna received me, feeble but jubilant. He was so choked with emotion that he was muttering gibberish phrases I could not understand. When I calmed him down and we drank the coffee, I reverently put the tattered saddle bag before him and said 'here is your treasure, Abouna, there pull it out". He fumbled with the bag as he pulled the cracked vellum, distorted with age and touched it lovingly raising it to his head. "Abouna", I cried "it is not a holy book!" "Ah, my child it is holy in the sense that it will provide new insight into the record of man" he murmured while touching it and gazing at it closely with his half blind eyes before he opened it. "It is a culmination of a lifetime dream. Now tell me and in detail how you found it".

I told him, keeping Boris out of the picture, but I knew that he was already well informed about my movements.

Abouna sighed. "you have paid a heavy price my child, it is sad that one has to give up the little happiness that comes our way once in a lifetime, especially at an age when sentiments are primordial"; he winked at me with his good eye as he said this, acknowledging that he knew about Boris, and before I asked him how he knew he said, wheezing and choking, "you know, I always read your mind, even at a distance, and to think that you have given me great happiness, and I only gave you pain and acted like a coward". "I could describe you with many epithets Abouna but cowardice is not one of them" I said. "Ah, my child, you remember the day you were accosted in a narrow alley of Jerusalem by the priest who brought you here, shocked and frightened. I had planned to tell you then the whole story, but when I saw you, young and fragile, my nerves broke and I have the crisis. For how could I brazenly tell you that you were spotted, spied upon, and proved genetically a Ghassanid, without your knowledge, but above all that I planned to ask you to go on an impossible mission. You see why my nerves failed, and then I was afraid that the shock would induce a heart attack or that you would go to the police, But then I knew you would not go to the police of the occupiers for help, you see I was not only a coward but a criminal who invaded your life and privacy without your knowledge.The only faint line of hope was that you would fall for the call of the unknown, for the mystery and adventure. And now that you have brought back the lost prophecy, a book which is responsible for turning two men of the church into criminals – the one who stole it and the one who is facing you, who had no right to play havoc with your life." Abouna's voice broke as he covered his face with his hands to hide the tears that ran from one of his eye. I was silent for he did not reveal anything new. He then continued "You thought that the attacks at appropriate times were feigned, but they were real, saving me from coming to the point of telling you the truth. Instead I played the game of a modern Syriac nationalist which made you believe I was trying to recruit you for the cause tut, tut, it didn't work but then I had a brilliant idea. I had spotted your Achilles heel, your obsession with ancient history and thus played the game of the Aramean civilization and its ancient gods. Again I said nothing. He continued "I set you on a perilous path – it all began a long time ago when I was named the bishop of this monastery and discovered the first part of the prophecy amongst our archives. I knew the story, which is part of the legendary history of this place of the young monk Behnam and the promise he gave to the bishop of Hira 1,400 years ago. Why did I feel the incessant urge to fulfill that promise? I do not know, it was like I was ravaged by fever and obsessed with finding the lost half.

I was in a dilemma until it dawned upon me to appeal to the Committee of Nine whose main aim was to preserve and revive the Chaldo/Assyrian/Syriac heritage. I did. Their response was quick and enthusiastic with an invitation to go to Sweden. I carried with me a copy of the first half and told them that the second half must be traced and recuperated. They agreed but then I threw a bomb and told them that when the lost half is found and the whole prophecy studied and interpreted by scholars, it had to be handed over to a descendant of Ghassan. The Committee was outraged at my proposal. They mocked and ridiculed me. "Why would we hand a precious piece of our heritage to Arabs? And to whom? A descendant of an extinguished insignificant dynasty of the 7th century at that." I swallowed the ridicule and the insults, instead I pleaded and haggled with them – the three Syriac members of the committee helped, but the other six Chaldo/Assyrians were adamant, for they had no historic debts to pay to Harith bin Jabla, being Catholics and not concerned with the Syrian Orthodox church.

I controlled my fury and prepared to return to Jerusalem empty-handed, but when I claimed the copy of the prophecy which they had started to study, they relented and informed me that they accepted my condition with some reservations but, oh my child, the memory of their proposals which you well know is still painful. Handing the prophecy to a Ghassanid was to be only a symbolic gesture, meanwhile they were willing to give the Ghassanid the right of veto on all matters concerning the prophecy. Legal ownership was to be given to our monastery in Jerusalem, but that was not an act of charity on their part for we did own the first half. Here Abouna paused, breathless. The worst

156

was to come, for they insisted that the Ghassanid I designate must be of *bona fide* authentic ancestry and that when the descent is proved he/she must recuperate the lost half of the prophecy with the help of their agents"! The last two conditions left me outraged and scandalized for in their cunning they calculated that I could not possibly accept and thus would give up the Ghassanid connection. I did not respond or react to their proposals but I spent two days and nights secluded in my hotel room in meditation and prayer. On the third day I informed them that I would accept their impossible conditions and my totally unexpected reply stunned them into silence.

Back in Jerusalem, with a very generous amount of money, transferred to a newly-opened bank account, I set about looking for a chimera, a live Ghassanid. I called two trusted historians who sifted the claims of families in Palestine, Lebanon, Syria and Jordan, that they believed they were of Ghassanid descent. Finally from sheer lethargy I chose those nearest to Jerusalem, the five clans in your village who claim to be descendats and set about finding a single unattached male or female from the clans, who had a sense of history and adventure. It was easy to spot you – you were single, of the right age, had studied and taught history in the village school, with a reputation of a nonconformist, a rebel. We gathered every detail about you. We even had a psychological profile prepared and yet, when I met you, you were different from the picture I had drawn of you in my mind from reading the files. We waited and waited, trying to prove your Ghassanid descent until the Ghassanid tombs were discovered by the famous Franciscan archaeologist. It was a miracle, my child. But that part of the tale you already know". He paused, tired but excited and when no reaction from me was forthcoming he called for coffee, to which both of us were addicted, raised his cup and said "I drink to your ancestors" for without them I would have been a poor parish priest in a Greek Orthodox church, instead of sitting on the throne of the Syriac bishop of Jerusalem. And, my dear child, I drink to you, the symbolic owner of the Chaldean Prophecy".

The long speck fatigued him but his face shone. Abouna", I said, "did you realize that you gave me a poisoned gift?" "Wait, wait, till this treasure be interpreted and studied by cryptographers, hieroglyphic scholars, Aramaic linguists, cosmologist, physicists historians, engineers, astronomers, the Nine have already called the specialists before you found it, because I assured them that you would". "Abouna", if the prophecy is what rumours say I don't fancy being disturbed, I am happy being on an insignificant planet which stands in the corner of a nondescript galaxy, I do not want to see the universe, I do not want to relinquish my life, my small ambitions to a vision I will be unable to bear". "Tut, tut" said Abouna you amaze me, you have found the prophecy, and now you are afraid to know its secrets". "Yes, Abouna, I am afraid, but tell me, you who knows something of the first half".

"You know, my child, I had spent my life lamenting my past and that of the nation, sorrow rules my life and pervaded my actions. I could not accept being uprooted from my homeland, now under Turkey and the movement of my family to Damascus, Beirut, Bethlehem and Jerusalem. I bewailed wastage, so many unfulfilled longings, futile hopes, illusory ambitions. I saw talent gone to dust with no chance to develop in the present environment and above all wars, waste, destruction, disillusion but above all I feared death, but when particles of the prophecy came to my knowledge I began to understand that there was no loss, no waste, no death – all was recycled. I began to lose my fear of death, my limited view expanded, but remember, the prophecy is a vast sea, of which I only glimpsed a drop, but you, my child, when the second half you recovered will be deciphered you will have a larger view of that sea".

"Abouna", you are a man of the Church and the prophecy I presume is counter to religious beliefs." "No, no, my child" he interrupted, "the prophecy engulfs all religions and all creeds, all the works of nature and man, there is no exclusion". "Does it speak of good and evil"? I asked. He answered slowly "action and reaction, good and evil, life and death, two sides of one, but for that we will wait to see what the

159

prophecy will tell. But let us talk of banalities. You need a rest after Urfa. I am very sensitive to this onslaught on your life. I plead guilty to persuasion and coercion and only beg that you will forgive an old man. Meanwhile all arrangements will be made for your travel to Stockholm to hand the prophecy to the Chaldo/Assyrian/Syriac Committee. Of course you know that by now the other seekers of the treasure plus the Turks realize that you whisked it from under their very noses and they will be looking for ways to share the cake with the Committee, but that is not in our hands'. "You mean the spies" I said bitterly. "I wouldn't call them spies" he said, they were academic people wanting the treasure for their institutes". I laughed loud and long at the thought that the CIA Kurd, and the British shoe-shiner, could be called academic, but I didn't want to open the wound nor face my grief over Boris, nor my guilt over outwitting and deceiving him and opted for silence.

I then saw Abouna shaking his head and mumbling incoherently as if struggling to say something and then suddenly his voice cleared as he said. "I kept you in the dark once and found a thousand justifications for doing so, but I cannot keep you in the dark again – although what I have to tell you is painful for you as well as for me. How shall I begin? You guessed that I was informed in detail about your relations with Boris, although I warned you not to have attachments while you are on the job but you fell in

160

love and it was then that I should have sent you a word but I refrained, I should have told you that Boris was one of us, a Syriac. His paternal great grandparents with many brothers fled Turkey to Russia in the 19th century because of ethnic and religious persecution where they formed a well-integrated community in Russia, producing scholars, generals, writers and diplomats, but they never forgot their roots or their ancient homeland. I interrupted him raising my voice "You mean that Boris was a double agent?" "Yes, my child, Boris was playing the double game". I was seething with a thousand sensations. Boris a double agent! Just like the British shoe-shiner!

Automatically, without thinking, I rose up to go. I wanted to run away from the thoughts that assailed me. "Sit, my child". Boris left Urfa soon after you left with the prophecy. He learned the news from us. I am told that he was stunned. He did not leave an address and I don't know his whereabouts. Nothing is perfect, my child. The joy in finding the treasure is mixed with this cup of sorrow for you and for Boris".

I did not utter a word. I left in silence and went home. How can I forgive what I have brought upon myself In Urfa, much as I loved him, I doubted his words and his actions and thought that he befriended me on the order of his superiors so that I may lead him to the treasure. He must be a very good actor I thought, but the words I doubted were genuine alas. He befriended me to protect me from all the sharks

161

surrounding me and I acted in a cowardly stealthy way, leaving him without a word of explanation. Why did I not give up the treasure and run away with him? Why didn't I throw Abouna and his wretched Syriacs to the wind? Is there a higher loyalty than that of the heart? By what malediction did I choose the camp of the treasure, drenched in duplicity, by what law did I choose loyalty to a double faced cunning priest instead of the one man I ever loved, questions like my lost dream that had no issue and no answer.

I continued in the twisted path I had chosen and prepared for the journey to Stockholm. I took possession of the prophecy again which was now in a Gucci bag instead of the smelly saddle bag which I clutched in my hands crossing the Allenby bridge where my luggage was minutely checked, except for the Gucci bag which I figured was due to some intervention along the line.

As a keeper of the prophecy I did not dare leave my hotel room in Amman, a city brimming with spies, nor even call my friends. On the plane at long last I knew I had two civilian bodyguards who did not introduce themselves.

My reception in Stockholm was very discreet. I met with the nine members of the Committee's modern young men, Syriac, Chaldean and Assyrian professors, scientists, lawyers and engineers, to whom I formally handed the Prophecy and they in turn returned it to me

162

in a symbolic gesture. The committee explained that they had contacted and sworn to secrecy twenty scholars form their community and told me with pride that no foreign specialist was invited. Scientists, astronomers, physicists, chemists, engineers, historians, specialists in Aramaic and Akkadian, astrologists, antiquarians and theologians who lived in Europe, America and Canada were invited with a copy of the whole manuscript. They were to meet once every three months during which they would discuss their findings and at the end of three years submit a joint first report. Further reports would follow.

To await three years for the mystery to be unraveled seemed an eternity, during which I rarely visited Jerusalem and resumed my teaching job, along with the routine of my old life in the village.

One day, in the second year, I received an urgent call from Jerusalem with summons form Abouna who was very ill and wanted to see me. I went, very worried with the certainty that Abouna would die before seeing the result of his long quest.

I was taken straight to his room which was darkened as the light irritated his half blind eyes and again that musty odour which struck me on my first visit assailed me. I was wondering if death had an odour. Abouna welcomed me by opening his eyes with difficulty and signaled for me to sit beside the bed. Near to his right ear for he has lost hearing in his left ear. I tried to smile and he talked in a low, broken voice. "Will you ever forgive me, my child for all the havoc I played with your life?"

Abouna", I said, "stop treating me as a victim", not knowing whether I blamed him or whether he was only a tool of fate. He resumed with difficulty. "When I first met you I was enjoying a miraculous awakening before death, which as you see, lasted a long time, your recovery of the manuscript was the greatest joy of my life – mark my words – the prophecy may be a blessing to mankind for it will provide a new insight into our existence on this planet. It may answer questions that have tortured the best minds in all ages. "Why are we here" I interrupted him teasingly. "My, my, Abouna! all this in a stolen manuscript". I repeat, stolen"! "Tut, tut, can you imagine the fate of the prophecy if it had stayed in Hira ? Stealing preserved it and remember that the half you recovered is in better condition than our half because of the care the monks at Mar Ephrem lavished on it but just the same it ended under a heap of trash.

I told Abouna that when I first opened the prophecy in my room I recognized only two words, the name of the thief, the bishop of Hira, I was afraid of handling it because the vellum was cracked. I tried to read with a magnifying glass, but in vain. Abouna cried 'the light is dim, the candle is giving out, but this small monastery is giving to the world what its future holds – you and I my child were instruments of the

164

divine to show that he is the alpha and omega". As he uttered these worlds his eyes were glazed and I was ushered out of the room.

When another call came after two days I rushed back to Jerusalem to find that Abouna was dead. I left the monastery after a last farewell to his body lying in state in the little church and retuned to my village to await the report and the summons to Sweden. A year later I received the report signed by the twenty scholars with a brief introduction which I read with fear and trembling.

BOOK II

The Report

Introduction:

Three years of deciphering the Chaldean Prophecy have led us, the twenty undersigned specialist, to the conclusion that human understanding of the works of God is beyond our mental and spiritual vision. Our limited interpretation of this prophecy is so fantastic that it changed our assumptions of the physical world and at times, led us to believe that all is illusion.

This prophecy is in reality a collection of different visions seen by prophets, high priests and mystics, recorded at different periods and collected much later into one manuscript, none of the authors or collectors is known, however one of the possible authors, is a certain Berossus (280 BC) who was a priest of Bel in Babylon and translated the text book on astrology into Greek. He later settled in the island of Cos, where many came to hear his prophecies. Another possible author is Jambaluchus (250-325 BC) founder of the school of neo-Platonism and author of a treatise on the mysteries of the Egyptians, Chaldeans and Assyrians. Another remote possibility is Abaris (400 BC), a magician known for long fasts and feats of levitation, reputed to have been the tutor of Pythagoras. The prophecy pictures a universe beyond logic and beyond reason. It erases the word impossible for our future decendants who will live in a mythical world, the world of our dreams, and brings back the myths and legends of our childhood, where on tapping a rock or reciting a formula "open sesame" the impossible occurred. Could it be that the tales of our childhood that strayed into our culture came from the future, by persons who lived in the future and told the tales that no one believed? At time, the prophecy appears as the work of discordant minds of mad men who ask us to shed the beliefs and habits of our lives, and to force us to enter into new dimensions. At times it gives hints that instead of many universes, there are many regions in one universe and that there may be many copies of ourselves in existence. On the other hand, it eliminates the fear of death for all is recycled and goes on forever, from the end of one universe to the birth of another. However, we must state that this very brief report deals only with the second half of the prophecy and covers hardly a third of its contents , which means it is incomplete. A full and complete report would need more than one lifetime of study. It is to be noted that these prophecies or visions were meant to be handled only by the high priests of Bel and not to be revealed to the public. The Chaldeans and Assyrians believed that everything was made of numbers which they endowed with a magical and sacred status, for example, Venus was number 19, the moon Was 30 and thus most of the visions were recorded numbers. The same path was followed by Pythagoras and his followers in the 6th and 5th century BC (569-470). For them "numbers are the measure of all things" cosmic order was based on numerical relationships, certain numbers and forms were imbued with mystical significance and they sought the inner meaning of nature through mathematical symbols. They discovered the role of numbers in music and applied the numerology to astronomy. This connection between musical and heavenly harmony was epitomized by the assertion that the astronomical spheres, inaudible to mortals gave forth music as they turned".

Numbers became prominent in the hermetic tradition that succeeded the Pythogorians, a tradition that goes back to one called Hermes Trismegistus, a fabled author of 42 books about the philosophy of ancient Egypt. The Hermetic view was affirmed in the middle ages by Parcellus (1490-1541) who stated that human life is inseparable from that of the universe and that the clay from which men are made was composed of every chemical element in existence. He spoke of the prevalence of the universal mind. Later, Gnostics and Cabalists constructed esoteric numerological roles, the devil was for example number 666.

The Chaldeans, authors of the prophecy, were proficient in the spheres of astrology, sooth-saying and magic, since remote ancient times. They foretold the fate of Alexander the Great on his return to Babylon from India. The priests of Bel pleaded with him not to enter Babylon but he did not heed their warning and thus met his tragic destiny.

The prophecy which is in our hands today went through many transformations as the visions were first in cuneiform carved on clay tablets and assembled much later by anonymous priests who transcribed the cuneiform tablets into ancient Aramaic, but new prophecies were added in each generation. The existence of the prophecy became well known but its contents were kept secret.

The prophets or seers were Bel high priests who through hypnotic trances saw the cycles of the future in images they expressed in numbers, at times by symbols, or figures or designs. The seers did not understand the strange visions they saw for they were not related to the world they lived in but they recorded the machines they saw in numbers and symbols and sometimes in crude designs.

The mysterious document was held in reverence and awe by the populace, an awe that persisted after the adoption of Christianity. And even though it did not accord with the new religious dogma, it was their sacred heritage and accorded a sort of ancestral worship. The Persian Sasanians overthrew lords of the Arab Lakhmids. Rulers of the kingdom of Hira and its native Nestorian Chaldean population were aware through vague rumours of the existence of the sacred Book. They were very eager to lay their hands on it, but they were met by denials of its existence and never succeeded in locating its whereabouts. The manuscript was kept hidden in a secret Chaldean monastery outside Hira, protected by ferocious guardians who spread the rumour that an agonized long and painful death awaited anyone who dared to put his hands on it, a prediction which was realized, but despite the guardianships and the malediction, the manuscript was stolen and surfaced in Edessa in the middle of the 6th century but only a few people knew that it was split with the first half in Jerusalem. The Chaldean keepers in Hira moved heaven and earth to regain the prophecy and kept a persistent search until the Arab conquest of Iraq in the 7th century. However, legends surrounding the prophecy survived its loss and rumours about its possible location reached academic institutions in both the oriental and occidental worlds. One of those romantic legends insists that it indicates in numbers the hiding place in Babylon of the treasure of Alexander the Great and that this was one of the reasons for its theft by the bishop, who on his death bed willed the prophecy to the king of Ghassan, the archenemy of the Lakhmids of Hira as an act of revenge. This is because the Lakhmids did not provide protection to the bishop from Persian persecution. The Committee of Nine fascinated by the tale of the treasure of Alexander, asked us to find the hiding place indicated in numbers by the high priest of Bel, but our cryptologists searched in vain. In the academic world it was known that it foretold the future, a fact arousing the interest of certain sections in intelligence services which dealt with telepathy and the paranormal for military purposes. Engineers in top secret sections heard rumours that the prophecy described machines of the future and were most eager to place their hands upon any blueprints or designs.

The following main themes that we deciphered from the manuscript were reconstructed by us, through inference, analysis, deduction and elimination, but mainly through pure imagination. Difficulties and obstacles apart, we had the privilege of bringing to the light questions man has been asking since he first gained awareness "Why are we here?" Is our existence planned, or is it an accident of fate? The prophecy addresses these questions and affirms that the "cosmos is controlled by a super intelligence who guides its evolution.

In general, the prophecy speaks of all things that are still in the beyond, in the form of ideas that have yet to become real. It is governed by a law of reincarnation running- through end and beginning, which brings about all phenomena in time, each step attained becomes the preparation of the next. God, who towers high above the multitude of all things, shapes beings to attain their specific nature in conformity with the great harmony. He creates conditions in which each receives what accords with his being, for each man must make a free choice according to his inner law and what is due to him, and what constitutes his happiness. God, the divine creative principle, the father, radiant energy, causes the beginning and begetting of all things.

Mystical thought which is the essence of the prophecy lies at the extreme opposite of rational thought. But it is not the mysticism that some confuse with the occult, paranormal and other fringe beliefs. The prophecies were results of mystical experience which is hard to convey in words, an overwhelming sense of being at one with the universe or with God, glimpsing a holistic vision of reality. Most mystics claim they can grasp ultimate reality in a single experience instead of the tortuous deductive sequence of the logical scientific method of inquiry. In such experience, boundaries between the self and the outer world vanish. The experience is a short cut to truth, a direct contact with ultimate reality. Mystical knowledge is attained all at once, there is no gradual path.

We would like to apologize for some repetitions in the themes that follow, due to the same vision seen by different high priests at different periods and as the cryptologists took pains in decoding each vision, we felt we must include them in spite of repetition.

Chapter VIII
THE REPORT - A: EVOLUTION

Biological evolution is one of the main themes of the prophecy, described by prophets and seers through hypnotic trances, in different unrelated periods, and recorded in numbers, astrological symbols, crude designs and figures. To give some coherence to these visions we have filled gaps by deduction, inference or just pure imagination. We cannot boast of submitting these visions to logic for the word logic as we know it does not figure in the prophecies. The seers recorded as a religious duty what must have seemed to them the height of unreality, the fantastic, the unimaginable, but we must keep in mind that they were high priests who had been trained in a severe discipline and waited long years before they were granted the privilege of seeing the past and the future. They do so in an altered state of consciousness in which bonds of time are freed and the mind sees the universe as it really is. The altered states of consciousness are used as energy fields, in which they see the whole cosmos where all times exist simultaneously. The trances could have been simulated by powerful drugs of which the priests alone know the secret that expanded their one-dimensional perception of time into myriad other dimensions and preceded by a long and rigorous training through fasting and physical and spiritual exercise coupled with the use of unguents, oils, perfumes and incense. The other possibility is time travel in teleportation machines through space and time, and in which they are physically moved into the past and future areas that they faithfully record.

The text that follows narrates different selected visions on evolution and mutation built on our own limited understanding of the numbers, designs and symbols in which the prophets expressed what they saw. In other words, it is our reconstruction of the vision of the Chaldean high priests.

The cosmos is controlled by a super intelligence "who guides evolution" and there is a law of evolution which directs the course of biological development over eons of time , too long to be measured but the process will not always be slow, sudden mutations occur regularly to hasten the process. The reasons for such mutations appear varied in the prophecy, geological movement of the planet, severe changes in the climate, or man-induced chemical or atomic wars, another is the erratic movement of heavenly bodies. All these induce radical changes in the environment which make it uninhabitable for humans, only mutations will enable the species to survive.

The internal working laws of the universe are constantly changing and evolving with the passage of time, for the entire universe is in a state of flux, with galaxies rushing away from one another at ever-increasing speed, the very structure of space and time are not fixed and inimitable. At times the prophecies lead us to believe perhaps erroneously that order in the physical world is based on an illusion.

Human intellectual powers are presumably determined by biological evolution. Our brains have evolved in response to environmental pressures. Some minds are poised to fathom the depths of nature's secrets, geniuses and visionaries occur in every generation.

The slow work of evolution is perceived only by a few, but when mutations occur, the whole population suffers its effects. Mutations occur because of changes in the environment which probably trigger changes in the body chemistry by the secretion of hormones. Environmental upheavals, such as rising sea levels which damage coastal cities, shift shore lines, move mountains and dry up lakes and rivers, but the worst devastation falls on coastal Cities in which the sea retreats, leaving ports miles inland. Extreme heat or extreme cold leads to the flight of populations to the interior hills and mountains, where new towns spring up. However, man has survived, despite the earth shaking and continents moving because of mutations

178

which change his behaviour patterns and transform his genetic make-up.

There is no chronology of mutations in the prophecy, but the major mutation described in detail was the last one because it was closest to the end. It occurred when the first baby was born with a large head, a small torso, short legs and long fingers. The baby was regarded as a monster but to the scientists an enlarged head housed an enlarged brain.

In time, the older species died out and the new species with not only large heads but large eyes, large noses and ears that protruded like those of a donkey. Animals too, went through a mutation and domestic animals, cats and dogs, were developing the gene for speech much to the delight of animal lovers.

The wombs of women however were too small for the large heads and Caesarean births became a dangerous hazard, leading to maternal mortality. Many women refused to bear children but for those who did, it was a painful sacrifice.

The authorities were forced to act quickly to raise the dwindling population which descended to near zero level with the result that researchers resorted to artificial birth and produced the 'jars', large glass containers with a degree of similarity to the womb. Artificial birth raised an outcry in part of the population, but this changed when they saw the babies healthier than those born naturally, nevertheless it brought a radical change to the style of living, parents desiring a child had to undergo Calvary in severe medical check ups to determine their suitability for parenthood before donating their eggs and sperms. The parents were entitled to visit the baby once every month to watch its development in the glass jar lined against the wall of the hall of the hatching farm. In the beginning the parents could choose the sex, ordering a boy or a girl like buying a kilogram of onions in the market, but when the balance of the population was threatened, for most of the orders were for boys, especially in the African, Arab and Asian regions, the parents were not allowed to choose and nature was left to determine the sex.

With the sex balance being restored, there loomed another disaster, the numerous tests on the foetus banished anomalies, malformations and diseased genes producing a perfect physical specimen which later turned into a nightmare. The so-called physical perfection was illusory and soon turned to an abnormality, for those perfect children had a deficient immunity and were not able to resist disease. Their very perfection was a handicap and the effect on the population was horrendous, the law governing the check up on the foetus was abrogated and it was allowed to grow naturally with minimum interference in its genetic make-up. The social structure of the new society was changed, for mothers relieved or grieved by the absence of child-bearing became aggressive and began looking for new horizons invading men's spheres which led to the break-up of many homes and the fragmentation of society.

Human form shown in crude designs in the prophecy is very, repulsive with faces verging on the square and out of proportion with the small bodies and the large, hideous nostrils, large eyes and long ears. The new forms however had enlarged sight and acute hearing and a very sharp sense of smell. The long, delicate fingers dealt with intricate machines and the legs lost their utility for walking was a rare occurrence, almost everyone possessed an individual flying vehicle.

Beauty and harmony had to follow the misshapen forms and this was reflected in architecture in small homes that replaced the apartment blocks. The houses had to have a certain orientation decreed by law, so as to capture the sun's rays and to be at an angle which harmonizes with the heavenly bodies above. The windows were slits to filter the light for the enlarged ultra-sensitive eyes. In contrast, public buildings which housed all kinds of machinery that sustained the life of the agglomeration were very large. Town halls used for administration and entertainment were also very spacious. Ideals of beauty had to conform to new criteria of the new evolved society. Public and private hygiene were strictly controlled for the enlarged noses were most sensitive to noxious smells. Traffic was controlled by a huge mother machine which regulated both private and public transport, street lighting, household electricity and heating. Fuel was replaced by sun rays in summer. In winter and in countries where the sun is shy in appearance, the sun's rays were captured and stored in containers and in countries of extreme cold, radiation was captured from the air.

The massive future utilization of the sun's energy reminded us of "sun worship" practised by different ancient civilizations and we wondered if this sun worship was a memory or a vestige of a time in the past or in the future when the sun was so harnessed. It is difficult to adjust our limited optic to the idea that past, present and future time run simultaneously.

The new evolved man, with his hideous shape achieved wonders with his enlarged brain, with eyesight that went beyond the limits we know, peeping into formerly closed doors of the universe, with his large nose that gave him a sensitivity to smell which outmatched that of cats, who recognized people by their smell, and his donkey ears which enabled to hear the earth murmur and tremble before an earthquake, or the irregular vibration of an air machine before a crash.

The mutation however did not pass so easily. It induced panic all over the planet with fear that humans were being metamorphosed into large-headed monsters coupled with "the panic over the climatic changes that preceded the mutation that drastically changed the land

and seascape, destroyed beloved cities with their skyscrapers and towers crumbling into dust. Many clung and refused to leave their ruined homes. However they were forced to abandon when the substructure failed, water, electricity and sewage broke down and man had to flee, despite his lamentation and regrets.

Human resilience in the miniscule bodies rose to the surface and man accommodated himself to the new home, new life by changing his sense of values and aesthetic criteria. The government helped by fostering and strengthening relationships within the family, especially between a mother and her glass jar child, "for at the beginning, mothers shunned the children not born from their wombs and treated them as belonging to the community rather than to themselves, especially as the intelligence of these children largely bypassed that of the parents, but with time this chasm was healed, especially as the majority of the population was now artificially born and with the same resilience; man began to regard his repulsive form as beautiful.

With the machines doing the bulk of the work, the people had plenty of free time, the government considering leisure could cause uprisings focused on playing on human vanity especially their love of clothes by spending incredible sums on research for creating new textiles. The new materials reacted automatically to temperature. The fibers changed according to the weather, cool in summer and warm in winter and were water-proof, but above all beautiful. The colours and prints were designed by artists in each region, with colours turning automatically bright as soon as the darkness fell which made night life a wonder as the streets sparkled with people shedding light like fireflies. Couture houses that catered for the three categories of human habitation made special materials and designs to suit the environment for those who inhabited space and for those who lived under the sea and under the earth.

For the world elite of governors and high officials jewelled threads were used and a man's status could be told by a glimpse at his clothes. Money had been of little use for centuries, commercial transactions and payment for work were by points in what resembled check books. They were given monthly according to the type and quality of work. Only very high graded workers could get sufficient points to buy the very expensive beautiful clothes which indicated their social status. Men wear as vainly as women, especially that both indulge in very bright colours and wear a lot of jewelry. Precious and semi-precious stones are mined from moons and stars by those who inhabit space and sent to earth where they are used for industry and medicine but above all for ornaments. Clothes could only be worn for seven days because the material programmed for heat and cold would disintegrate and give sounds as they cracked before they are given to the special warehouses to have them recycled.

Selecting and buying clothes every seven days kept people happily busy for the bright coloured clothes and shimmering jewels compensated for their miniscule forms and drab lives, but besides the pleasure they gave to individuals they were used for display in parades, sport events; festivals and concerts, which the authorities arranged twice a month with the idea that happy crowds, parade with banners, drums and music were a psychological necessity for humans and act as a catharsis for the accumulating resentments.

The learning process was audio-visual in which the far-sighted eyes and the large protruding ears helped. Laboratories in which the students learned all the new techniques served as classrooms but the educational process continued through the night when each student at bedtime, put a disc given to him daily under his pillow to instruct him during sleep. At the end of the elementary cycle, children were distributed to specialized schools according to their aptitude and a caste system developed based on higher and lower intelligence.

The machines that captured the past were used in the educational process but they were few and expensive, based on the principle that all time exists simultaneously and nothing is ever lost, every past event and every word uttered in the universe is there lurking around us to be caught and brought to light; It took myriad centuries for man to invent the machine that could penetrate and capture the past alive, but its use was very restricted for the shapes of the ancestors were seen as grotesque by the evolved humans who saw them in the rare recessive creatures born on rare occasions with the physical appearance of the ancestors and whom the authorities put in a special zoo to protect them from the hostility of the public.

Highly specialized scholars and professors were given special permits to view a live past era of their specialty but the farther the era receded in time the more difficult for the machine to capture. Historians and archaeologists who were privileged to see the past were continually under shock for reality was different from what text books told about a Roman legion in battle or Greeks shouting their war cry. Many were grieved to see that the cities they idealized Ur, Thebes or Athens did not conform to the image in history books.

Schools differed in various regions with programmes for sea and sky, inhabitants different from those on earth, but all had to follow a compulsory programme on 'civic education' established by the world government, and aimed at fostering fellowship between men. It taught that man is unique: extensive Space probes and visits have not succeeded in finding another Species but the super intelligence that created him, endowed him with the capacity of biological evolution with a brain evolving into a progressive higher awareness but man alone is sustained by fellowship with other men, a fellowship second only to the love of God. Old religious fanatics complained that "civic education" was becoming a sort of, universal religion.

The educational system however was constantly alert to any physical changes in the students or in their behaviour patterns for signs of the evolutionary process. Accordingly they were constantly measured and scanned, for the scientists were expecting a slow evolutionary development or a mutation, especially in the people who lived on and under the sea and those in the sky. As evolution develops in reaction to environmental changes and the new, unfamiliar environment of man inhabiting the sea and the sky would surely lead to physical changes which will help him to adapt to life in the new sphere; a mutation that would enable the people who inhabit space to develop wings instead of arms and those who lived in the sea to develop scales on their skin.

Illness was considered as a retribution for the patients misdeeds in past reincarnations and had to be suffered as such. Treatment was in clinics surrounded by beautiful landscapes with running water and lush green gardens. Walls in the buildings were painted to simulate seas, lakes and mountains. Music was a major healing element so was poetry read by mellow voices. Healing was mainly achieved by restoring harmony

187

through massive doses of energy given to the patient from a public reservoir of energy fed by the contribution of the public as an obligatory tax. Friends and relatives sent doses of energy, instead of the usual flowers and chocolates of the past.

Two luxury items in the past, gems and perfumes, were now used for healing by inducing meditation. Hospitals kept huge trays of large gems so that the patient could handle and rub them in his hands and on his temples emeralds cured headaches, rubies bad digestion, diamonds eyes diseases, part of the cure was the radiation of the gems and the pleasure they induced in the patient. Perfumes made in special laboratories in upper Egypt where the ancient Pharaonic formula for their composition was discovered, were exported to hospitals over the globe and again they gave pleasure to the senses besides the cure. Doctors were not only chosen for their skills but their good looks and honeyed manners which were part of the cure.

Terminal illnesses that preyed on pre-mutation man were eradicated but the felicity did not last as new deadly diseases broke out every few decades due to climatic changes which lead to the emergence of new breeds of bacteria or parasites and the cycle of research and eradication went on.

Illness was detected by the patient himself before its onslaught through the machine he-carried on his-person at all times. .The machine was given to every baby out of the glass jar as a birth right. It recorded data on his health from birth to death and sounded a small alarm when it detected a coming indisposition. The alarm necessitated seeing a doctor who on manipulating the machine could diagnose the illness, a red button for emergency if pressed brought a mobile hospital to the door.

As cities disappeared, evolved man split his habitat into three different spheres - land, water and sky. Those who clung to old traditions lived on the land in small agglomerations, grouped around large buildings that housed the machines, which sustained the life 'of the community, others burrowed underground and lived in semi-darkness, driven by the sensitivity of their enlarged eyes to the light in miniature homes with shafts for light and air grouped around the central machines. Their occupations were the study of the interior of the earth, tectonic geology, seismology and movement of the plaques and mining. Those who lived on water, seas, rivers and lakes lived either on house boats or under the water in small submarines grouped around a large mother submarine which had all the amenities. Their task was sea farming and studying water species not known to man before. The third group were space farers who lived suspended between earth and sky in large satellites, many of them had first lived in Colonies on the moon but found that too costly. They were mainly descendants of the first astronauts. Their tasks were mining the meteorites and manning missions of discovery to the far ends of space. The different environments in which people lived resulted in marked differences as the view from the sky and the sea differed from the View of those who were earth bound, but the one and unique world government with its strict-laws kept the human race together and permitted rivalry only in the fields of technology, sport, discovery and artistic achievements.

The machines that sustained life for the three habitations were based on land in large public buildings. Machines regulated all aspects of human life. The machine houses were manned by cosmologists, sociologists, ethnologists, astronomers, physicists, engineers, architects and artists, directly under the control of a commissioner of the world government.

The machines did the bulk of the technical and manual work in the three environments for the small evolved bodies were not capable of doing the work of former generations. The number of the population was kept in control. Single parents did not exist. The law gave the child the right to have two parents.

As the machines did the bulk of the work many venues for enjoyment were open and allowed men to indulge in their favourite pursuits, space exploration was a major pastime for all, not only for those who lived in space for the hope of finding another species akin to man although dim, persisted, many kept up the search in the belief that an exact copy of our planet and ourselves existed in a far-away galaxy.The major pursuit. of cosmologists was the exploration and mapping 'of the dark area which makes more than eighty percent of matter in all the universe and which does not emit or reflect light, but collapses into filaments or slender thread and then into clusters forming a gravitational scaffold into which gas can accumulate and stars can be built. Astrologists indulged in their favourite hunt for life forms on the different planets and geologists were continuously examining geological changes in the planets. As logical constancy was thrown to the wind, all possibilities were open besides space exploration, great enjoyment was derived from frequenting the ancestral halls in each agglomeration where on a large screen they could see selected scenes of vanished cities with their skyscrapers, towers, markets and homes.

The great mystery was the time machine that captured live events of the past and of the future but access to these machines was limited to a small aristocracy of intellectuals and philosophers who had contributed to the welfare of humanity through their inventions, discoveries, research, exploration, or through their books.

The public always avid for mysteries, pestered the government about the time machine for they wanted the same treatment accorded to the intellectuals and philosophers but even amongst the elite viewing the past events was according to their grade of enlightenment. Those at the lower level could see and hear the live events of the last few centuries, higher grades could see the ancient past or even recede further to the stone age but only a very few could see the emergence of our planet out of gas debris and chaos.

We do not know at what stage in fluid and reversible time the production of food by natural means came to an end. Nourishment was now produced from air by machines of all sizes, for restaurants, families or even individual use. The machines came with a pamphlet which explained which buttons to touch and which formula to recite in the little microphone to obtain the desired meal listed in the brochure. The machines were distributed by the government, and responded only to the authorized voice of the owner. The machines were popular in space and sea but most people on land kept clandestine agriculture and animals and preferred to cook their own food but this was frowned upon.

After several epochs of felicity and peace man became restless and resentful of the machines that sustained and controlled his life and so he rebelled against this state of semi-perfection and in land, sea and sky he broke the laws and destroyed the machines and reverted back to a savage, lawless life and a chaotic uncontrolled existence, but these periodical revolts were crushed and tamed by the 'elders who forced man to rebuild what he had destroyed. The prophecy does not enumerate the thousands of times this pattern of building, destruction and rebuilding occurred, however these regressions which lasted for decades did not stop the course of evolution, through the constant growth of man's awareness.

CHAPTER IX
THE REPORT - B: INCARNATION

Immortality and infinity, human dreams in the realm of the impossible, appear as facts in the Chaldean prophecy through incarnation, but man in his limited biological existence can neither fathom, digest, nor accept the idea of immortality and therefore it is veiled from him.

Reincarnation or the transmigration of souls is a very ancient belief which figures in many religions, mainly Buddhism and in the teaching of philosophers from Plato, Plotinus to Pythagoras. The idea is that each entity that ever lived on this earth goes through the process of constant change until its final purification when it can enter and merge with the body of God, the Creator.

The Pythagoreans in the 6th century BC believed that the elevation of their social status in the next world could be guaranteed by rigorous adherence to their code of conduct in the present one, eventually the cycle of birth and death might be broken by their sublimation into eternal union with the gods or oneness with the cosmos. The Pythagorians were seeking the divine harmony of the world in order that they might become one with it. The Hermetic tradition derived from 15 anonymous treatises written in the first three centuries and ascribed to the Egyptian God Hermes Trismegistrus succeeded the Pythagorians in this belief. In the Middle Ages the Hermetic View was widely spread by Parcellus (1490-1541). Reincarnation with its central idea that the soul is eternal haunted man's imagination throughout the ages but man with the one-dimensional perception of time trapped in his brain could not conceive of any existence before his birth and science was skeptical and yet there are areas in which people recognize their past reincarnations like some Tibetan Buddhists, others have recollections or certain affinities with animals or trees.

With the skepticism of scientists and the reservation that our interpretation of the prophecy is correct, the picture that emerges is that the number of souls created at the beginning is finite and remains the same until the end. No new souls are created, which means that each soul goes through inestimable reincarnations while the number of people on this planet earth is the same from beginning to end. The explosion in the population and the variation in number is attributed to entities, who are returning more frequently, and to the number of people who, in certain epochs, are reincarnated into animals and plants. The idea that each human soul has been going through eons of time and that it is as old as the universe or time itself is frightening to say the least. However the mental limitation of man is his protection, but above all he has a free choice to progress or to regress and as such he chooses each of his reincarnations according to the past one and enters by his free choice, into suitable biological groups, clans, families or races, where biological heredity fits in with the state necessary to his present development.

Reincarnation with its constant death and rebirth in an everlasting circle of annihilation and creation is difficult to accept as a process of which we are part and in which we see a shadow of the law of retribution or the law of balance and justice, for no deed or thought of man is ever lost or remains without consequence, everything is recorded in the invisible parts of the universe. In each reincarnation we pay for the last one and prepare for the next, until our slate is clean, all debts paid, we then become candidates for oneness with the cosmos and for entry to the realm of God.

As incarnation moves forward it can also fall backwards into criminality and low living, this regression can arrive at a point where the entity is metamorphosed into an animal or a plant, but however low the entity sinks it rises again, having gained something from the experience, it begins to move forward but the span of time it will take to reach purification will take a plethora of cycles of existence.

To those who believe in it, incarnation brings comprehension and consolation for it explains death, suffering depression and illness, good and bad fortune according to the law of retribution and yet it is man's will that is the decisive factor for it determines the number of his reincarnations, his freedom to take his own life or that of others, except that he will have to pay the heavy debt with thousands of incarnations. The fear of a thousand lifetimes put an end to the practice of suicide so prevalent in past generations.

The prophecy often mentions the "creatures of light" or "people in white", who are entities which have completed their full cycles of existence, they have escaped the wheel and are purified, but before returning to merge with the creator, they opt to remain on earth to help their fellow 'men. The "creatures of light" appear in every period and in every generation as ordinary, humble people, peasants, workers, housewives, teachers, doctors or priests. They flow with goodness and lighten the burdens of those around them. They help, comfort and console the needy, the sick, the depressed and shed light wherever they go.

We do not know when the belief in incarnation took hold of the people of the future, but we do know it became widespread when the time machine, which captured the past and the future, was invented. At first the invention was kept secret from the public for the world government considered the impact would sweep all the archaic beliefs which people held on religion, morals and philosophy and would overthrow the social structure, but the government could not keep the secret forever and when the news spread, man understood that he is as old as time, as old as the universe and that he, a living entity has died and was reborn hundreds and hundreds of times. He looked upon his present life as a stepping stone but that he can choose to have a better one in the next. He began to understand that injustice, suffering, disease, wastage and loss were payments for the errors of a past life and yet he was not permitted access to the time machine. It was given only to the top few to see their past lives. The prophecy does not indicate how these men of the future reacted to the eradication of the fear of death and adjusted their lives with the view of choosing their next birth in a suitable biological environment or to return again to their own family circles.

Those on the top who have reached the highest grade of enlightenment were given the privilege of seeing their past incarnation with the myriad lives in different ages, a dangerous venture. For one of the foremost engineers of the globe and one of the builders of the time machine lost his reason and attempted to commit suicide when he saw a black cobra as one of his past incarnations. The shock of the past lives was

198

too much even to those of the sharpest intellects, which lead the government to prohibit seeing one's past.

If capturing the past was allowed for the very few, capturing the future was a taboo except for the seven elders who governed the regions of the world for they are strong enough in spirit to see the end of all things.

The impact of incarnation, although widespread over the seven regions, did not penetrate certain pockets and enclaves which rejected the idea, veiled the reality from their evolved brains and clung ferociously to the old belief, that life is finite, mourned death as the end of all things and scoffed at the law of retribution. Some of those that held fast to old beliefs were famous artists and writers with followings in their areas of habitation. The regional governments did not interfere with them because of their intellectual standing but when they started to open private schools to indoctrinate the children, the authorities prohibited their public appearance and closed down the schools.

The effect of reincarnation on art and literature was calamitous with a dampening effect on creativity for how would a poet react to a world where loss, mourning and lamentation are no more used? will the poet sing the joy of infinite, eternal existence or will he lament the boredom and the horror of an existence in which we are trapped? Will he long for old days with their fears and suffering? Will he pine for a definite

finite death? Will the meaning of life change if we are condemned to live forever? Questions the prophecy evades. Moreover we could not decode the visions on art and philosophy which we hope will be deciphered in the future.

The belief in reincarnation did not exclude the beliefs and practices of the various religions for man is free to choose the path he follows. Some religious fanatics were overjoyed, hoping that the time machine would allow them to see their prophets and to hear them teaching, opposing religious zealots cried that to do so was a sacrilege. The dispute was ended by the government who decreed that viewing the prophets was prohibited.

The effect of decoding the prophecy on reincarnation was invigorating to some of us on the Committee, so we started to play lightly and question many of its themes. What is the relationship of the law of retribution with the Greek goddess Nemesis who personified retributive justice? 'Did God make of our planet an experimental research center for the whole universe? How far can human awareness grow? How superior are our minds to those of animals and plants, for in the last analysis research has not given us a clue of how trees feel about death. Is a cat aware of its own death? Does the stream under our window lament its coming dryness, its extinction? We questioned biological progress. Who knows whether humanity passed through periods of regression? Are we descended from monkeys? Or are monkeys and chimpanzees regressed humans? Is there evolution in reverse? Who will, guarantee that the future man does not fall victim to his arrogance when he knows that he is not simply a passenger in one lifetime, but a passenger in thousands of lives? Who will stop his arrogance when he knows that he, the little nondescript human is the howling wind, the raging sea, the shining stars? That he is the universe, and when the mandate of this universe is over he will participate in the creation of a new universe, because he is part of God the Creator.

The possible answer to the questions that troubled us as we struggled probing the prophecy was the link between evolution and incarnation. For only after the mutation that enlarged the human brains, that the veil was raised from the mystery and man became capable of understanding incarnation. God does not burden humans with things beyond their capacity. As man had to accept his changed physical form he now had to accept realities deeper and more subtle than he ever dreamed of.

Work on travel forward and backward in time, was going on for many generations. The high priests of Bel who saw past and future visions in an altered state of consciousness travelled physically to the past and the fixture in teleportation time machines and recorded what they actually saw in both spheres. Many prototypes of time machines were constructed and destroyed across the ages because 'of anomalies and defects as they were not in tune with the environment. The machine that finally made it was partly built by a quirk of chance when an engineer thought of using the quantum mechanical particles, the building blocks of the universe which had the ability to change from solid to wave form according to barometric pressure, atmospheric ionization or reaction to incidents surrounding it. When envious colleagues, who were working for so long unsuccessfully, asked him how he did it he answered: "In the beginning when space and time did not exist, God created the universe out of nothing. I, in, my ignorance of a beginner, lamented the energy and the large sums of money wasted all these years in building a teleportation machine. It was imperfect and I thought there must be a simple solution as I was gazing at a fig tree in the garden of the Institute, so lush, its very greenness showed an intensity of joy, which one of my dead engineer friends possessed and suddenly, it flashed upon me that he was incarnated in that tree. The words he told me one day, while talking to his colleagues who were building the teleportation machine, came clearly back. "Look at these fools, wasting energy and money, while all they have to do is to use the building blocks of the universe!" And that was that. If the blocks are good for the universe then they are good for the time machine!"

We were convinced that the Chaldean high priests did travel on these machines from their graphic descriptions and that they actually talked with the people of the future.

Curiously, the teleportation machines were dropped from the last part of the prophecy. They were outdated and replaced by the- "Holy of Holies", the time machine that captures the past and the future and projects it on the screen; it is described as very large and housed in special buildings, in specific areas at certain angles to the heavenly bodies. Seeing the future was strictly forbidden. The past was organized according to centuries or subjects, a button pressed could project a scene on a large screen in the hall.

The authorities who at first prohibited scenes of human ancestors, relented, and decided to show the ancestors slowly and gradually in an effort to educate people about evolution and how it changed the human form as the earth also changed its appearance.

At first the public was shocked. They could not 'believe what they saw, they booed, they screamed and stamped their feet, some fainted, others stampeded to get out - they closed their eyes, for they were frightened and disgusted, by the giant devils parading on the screen with their small heads, big bellies, in primitive vehicles and flying machines, but gradually they got used to seeing the giant devils who were their ancestors and they started to laugh at their awkwardness, at their long dangling legs and languid walk and found it all very amusing.

203

Ironically, they found the scenes of the past not only amusing but highly entertaining for they assured them of their own superiority and good fortune in comparison with the primitive savages who drove primitive machines and cooked their own food.

This period of felicity was shattered, when by error of judgment, scenes from World War I were projected on the screen. The diminutive people, who never knew wars, saw masses of young men in uniform killing other young men in uniform in battles on land, sea and air, on the orders of their generals, kings and presidents. They could not comprehend that the government which had bred, fed and educated these men had sent them to be slaughtered. How could a government order young men to kill and be killed? And how could the young men accept such orders like sheep? "No, no", they screamed, they rioted, destroyed the hall, cursed the government. "We cannot be descended from such savages. They are not our ancestors!" Experts and professors tried to explain war, but in vain". "Why were they bred like chickens to be killed?" The world government which had succeeded in eradicating war could not find one plausible explanation to give.

The Time machine that captured the past and the ordained future of the whole universe was now well known to the public who had access to selected areas of the past. It was totally prohibited after the last riot when battle scenes were shown. There was however a part of the secret machine that captured the past reincarnation of the individual but did not function for future incarnations. For while the entity is living, its future is not fixed, it is in a state of flux, depending on its comportment and free choice in this present existence.

The only people authorized to see their past were the seven elders and the governors of the seven regions, for they alone had the enlightenment to view their plethora of incarnations. The enlarged evolved brains of people were not capable of taking the shock; scientists who built the machine refused to see their past, besides to capture the path of one life amidst millions of years was a complicated process and very costly. As to the elders who have this privilege or malediction, no one knows if they see their past lives – it is a state secret!

The public who now enjoyed and reveled in the entertainment of seeing ages past was repelled by the individual time machine. Most people, even if they were offered the chance, did not want to see their past lives and shatter their present identity. Vestiges of old atavistic feelings and instincts still lived in the new man with enlarged heads. They longed for comfort, for coziness, for a limitation; For they felt that man had gone beyond all boundaries.

The elite, however, kept stretching their horizons with new inventions and new discoveries in a never-ending trail.

CHAPTER X

THE REPORT – C: WORLD GOVERNMENT

A world government, the culmination of an ancient human dream appears as a reality in the future, but it took unmeasured time for its fulfillment, after stages of instability and chaos, and was imposed by necessity on the survivors of the last and 25th atomic war. The destruction was global and the few survivors had no alternative but to group together and thus the world government was born.

The prophecy records so many visions of future war of which we were able to decipher only the last four: wars of minorities, wars of fuel, wars of water, and atomic wars of space.

The wars of minorities described as a fire running through a dry forest, took place in many sections of the globe, for reasons of religion, race and ideology. The first was a spontaneous rising by a religious minority, followed by other minorities who fought for different reasons. There was nothing common between them, except that they were minorities fighting oppressive majorities. Some of these wars succeeded, and split mighty countries into small autonomous groupings. Others failed and were crushed, wiping the minority out of existence through massive genocides. The wound left by these wars was so deep that the scars it left forced the world government much later to take severe legal measures against any friction between minorities and majorities, cases of discrimination, humiliation and exploitation of minorities were considered as crimes of high treason, punishable by exile with hard manual labour in the most remote corners of the earth.

Minority wars caused disruption of large countries, followed by social upheavals which lead to "Energy" or "Fuel" wars with governments trying to lay their hands on the diminishing petroleum and coal resources and the last dying forests. Strong countries agressed each other, while the weaker countries with sources of energy who tried to resist, were crushed and colonized and their energy was taken over.

New sources of energy had to be discovered, mainly the sun which resulted in an exodus from countries in the north of the globe to the lands of Africa and Asia and Latin America. The natives resisted; but the new immigrants claimed sunlight as their birth right-even though they were born in the cold. Tapping the sun rays was nothing new but it was now replaced by the solar wind which produced most of the world's energy. Meanwhile, another major problem was looming, the scarcity of water and the rush to sun lands now became translated into a rush to water lands and wars for water sources ensued with most countries joining the melee, but the small, weak countries paid the price by being almost wiped out of existence.

The wheel of war kept turning for after the rush to sunlands and waterlands it was now a rush for a place in the stars.

The last war of space, known as the 25th atomic world war was longer and deadlier than the twenty four atomic wars the world has known and the three preceding wars of minority, energy and water. Rivalry in space which began as early as the 20th century led to world wars in which not only highly industrialized countries took part but poor underdeveloped countries joined for a part in the space cake. Claims and Counterclaims for ownership of parts of Space went first to the International Court for Arbitration but no settlement ensued, after which the contestants went to war in what was known as the most destructive and the last atomic war. It was a period of lost hope, for the space probes found no sign of life and the colonies that some countries established on the moon and on Mars at great expense were a complete failure. The settlers packed their bags and went to live in the large Satellites that were built to house them; only a few returned to earth. The stage was set for wholesale global destruction with the small nations who had clandestinely acquired the atomic bomb joining the melee. The first victims were the cities which had already suffered from climatic changes. Most of them vanished by the end of the war. The prophecy describes toppled towers, ruins and dust where no greenery would grow. A period of darkness followed with floods in some areas and desertification in others until the descendants of the survivors of the 25th atomic war emerged to regroup and create an alternate to the past, in a new way of life for they had absorbed the lesson and the world government was born for the earth had become very small with speedy travel and instant communication. The globe was divided into seven regions based on geographical, traditional and cultural lines when the cryptologists decoded from numbers the names of countries in each region, we were surprised to find that many countries do not figure in the map of the future, mainly the countries built on theocracy.

The world constitution which was projected on screens on the facades of public buildings - started with the ominous words "Man is not born biologically equal, but equal before the law. Equal opportunity to education, labour, and pursuit of mental and physical equilibrium, are his birthright" followed by commitment to the eradication of wars which plagued men through their history. "War is not born in the minds of men: and therefore cannot be eradicated from the minds of men". War is a basic instinct of aggression engineered for primitive man's survival but as man's awareness progressed, this instinct has become redundant and superfluous. No one so far has succeeded in eliminating war but if it cannot be eliminated it can be channeled. 'The world government decided to divert this basic instinct of aggression into venues that benefit humanity instead of destroying it. Many fields are open to citizens of the world capable of absorbing this aggressive energy; exploration of the farthest galaxies, mapping the dark area of the universe, building new travel machines ten times quicker than the speed of light, farming the seas, probing the depth of the oceans, rescue missions for travellers on land, sea and sky, moving mountains, building new pyramids, digging tunnels, researching new technologies, creating harmony, competing in all kinds of sports, composing music, creating beauty, writing poetry. Rivalry between the seven regions will be a competition for excellence and, as such, songs will be heard over the land, sea and sky instead of war cries.

All world citizens had the obligatory duty of giving one year of their lives between the ages of 18 to 25 to voluntary public service, in any of the above fields, according to their aptitude.

The seven elders that govern the world are chosen because of their very advanced mental and spiritual evolution. Their heads are larger than normal and they communicate with each other by telepathy.

They do not involve themselves in administration which is the domain of the regional assemblies with representatives elected according to the number of the population who appoint the consuls or regional governors. World citizens are encouraged to go beyond their latent energies and for the first time in history, humanity enjoyed a permanent peace. The animals profited from new laws against their torture or their slaughter and the earth was refreshed and was very green. The world resources were controlled and distributed equally between regions.

Continuous search for new sources of energy was a main target for the world government but the surprise above all surprises was the obvious one, man himself was energy, as one day the chief engineers in a northern region woke up to the fact and said to everybody's indignation, that this human source had to be utilized. The scientists who were scandalized rejected and scoffed at the idea of using man's physical body as an object to produce fuel, but research proved that man's inherent energy could be harnessed to drive a vehicle, one can sit in a flying machine and drive it with one's own body or energy field.

Rescue patrols or missions were one of the hardest and most dangerous, a citizen of the world could undertake only if he is in excellent physical and mental condition. Missions patrolled the skies and penetrated into deep space to rescue trapped and floating ships and lone astronomers in their flying machines. Patrols scanned the seas in sea farming areas. The rescue missions gave a sense of global security for the government esteemed that saving a human life was worth the large amount of money spent on these operations and strengthened its basic program on human fellowship.

The robotic machines which dominated the world for ages with house robots which recognized a human mood and robotic cars were now replaced by a new generation of smaller and more concise machines suitable to the diminutive people. The latest was the new flying machine which on pressing a button projected a tunic with wings that fitted the individual and when pressing several buttons would soar above the town on the energy of the rider as fuel. Such machines were only for short distances, for long distances there were many types of public flying machines. Ground vehicles disappear from the prophecy, as travelling was done solely by air. Another-was the "food machine" which was restricted at first to the few high officials, researchers and travellers who had no time or means for producing food, but was later distributed by the government to the public at large.

Most machines were activated by special formulae spoken to a small microphone, but the surprise was that the formula was familiar to us from the fairy and jinn tales of our childhood "Open sesame ", a relic and a vestige of time long past that clung to man's minds, a fossil from the time when their remote ancestors murmured the formula to open the caves of treasures of their myths but the "cliche" or residue was a reassuring link with the distant past of humanity, and yet the question always loomed: were our myths and legends vestiges of what visitors from the future actually described, but as no one believed them they turned into myths and tales?

With thousands of very advanced machines produced in workshops all over the world and well received by the public, it was the time machine that caused headaches for the government when certain scenes were first shown in town halls: the first screening was not of people but of unfamiliar landscapes, large rivers that were now little streams; huge coastal cities swallowed by the sea, deserts in places which were once very green. The reaction of the public 'was unexpected: at first there was a hushed silence and then they broke into an animal-like howl when they saw the Mediterranean as it was once. They could not believe it to be the same small lake they had now, but the howl turned into stamping of their little feet and cries when the government decided to show them human beings, the elongated fat forms of their ancestors with their dangling legs, and the two holes they had for eyes inspired them with horror as they shouted, ugly, ugly – they hooted, booed, jumped up and down and cursed. The shock that they are descended from these forms must be like our reaction when we see monkeys as our presumed ancestors. In some regions the reactions were more violent, for they wanted to destroy the machines and broke into riots. The regional consuls met and agreed that it was a failure of the school system which did not teach properly how radically the earth itself had changed its look and how the present human forms were developed after several mutations.

A long time passed before the elders judged that the time was propitious to open the town halls again for selected visions and episodes of the past. The reaction now was totally different, the diminutive people laughed at the awkward movements of their ancestors, especially their walk compared to their own quick hopping and they wondered aloud, how could they see with their small eyes and ah their small noses and ears. They were highly entertained by seeing their daily lives working, quarrelling, making love. Scenes of wars and atrocities were prohibited, but as we described before, when battles of World War I were inadvertently shown, all hell broke loose.

Attendance at these halls of entertainment turned into a sort of addiction for the past, which made some people unhinged, the government reacted by restricting attendance to once a month when long queues formed before the halls. If the halls were sometimes closed for machine repairs it caused protests and riots, reluctantly put down by the police.

Many people clamoured to see their own past, which was prohibited as very dangerous for their mental equilibrium especially if they saw their inanimate incarnations – like rocks or star dust –but those who clamoured most were the enclaves of old religions who said it was their right to see their prophets but their plea was refused again and again. The Buddhists with incarnation inherent in their breed did not join the protest.

The great beneficiaries of the time machine were historians, archaeologists and anthropologists who were assigned special halls to view areas of their specialties projected.

No aspect of life was more dominated by machines than households, for the machines watched over the children, prepared the food and left housewives free to take public jobs. Each household possessed a flying machine, kept on the flat roof, which replaced the outdated robotic cars used by past generations.

The machines gave people leisure, but plenty of headaches for the government which was alert at all times for signs of non-adaptation to the new age; any manifestation of lethargy, stagnation or protest sounded the alarm. Reactions to permanent peace and easy living where most material desires were attained led to pockets of dissenters and rebels who revolted against the banality of living. Most rebellions were by people who inhabited space or the sea for in those two confined environments it was easy to revolt.

The Elders realized that with machines making the impossible possible, a breakdown of the system of religions and morals, reaction was inevitable. Pockets of followers of the old religions joined together in an ecumenical gesture, Hindu and Buddhist priests with Cardinals, Imams and Rabbis from all regions protested, stamped their feet with anger and hopped together while they wrote a manifesto to the elders abhorring the aberration of morals, and insisted on the return of religion. Their adversaries followed with a manifesto of their own to the elders claiming they did not need the intervention of religious middlemen, for they had a direct access to the creator and they were responsible for their own morals in preparation for their future reincarnations which they hoped would be better. This made priests; imams, monks and rabbis even madder for they may be losing their livelihood and yet to their joy and surprise their old religions survived evolution and the onslaught of machines. The government dealt with the restlessness in two ways; they first sent waves of energy which calmed rebels for a time and then they offered them the challenge and adventure of voluntary rescue missions, for there were frequent accidents in both sea and sky. The motto for rescuers was "save one human life, you save the whole human race The rescuers repaired satellites and space ships damaged by rushing meteorites and above all

217

rescued the men mining metals on the meteorites or the floating passengers from flying machines who were ejected before a crash wearing special obligatory suits for all travellers which inflated and threw passengers into the void before a crash. The passengers pushed buttons on the suit to indicate their position but sometimes had to float many days before rescuers carried them to a mother ship standing by.

Warnings of disaster for those living in submarines gave them time to put on special suits which inflated on touching water and emitted sounds for rescuers. Both air and sea suits were life sustaining with oxygen, flash lights and food pills. They are also protected automatically against radiation and cold. The hardest task for rescuers was for those who lived underground for they had to reach the shafts before the soil movement blocked their way.

Rescuers were hailed as heroes of the world. Their exploits were material for writers, artists and their saga was sung by poets; as they replaced the scientists and technicians, heroes of former generations. The Elders had their own major preoccupations, the first, a clean globe without pollution was already achieved, for there were no heavy industries and fuel, petroleum and coal were long out of use. The second was to increase the world supply of energy, to be tapped in the future need. For this purpose epistles were sent to all men who are nothing but energy, requesting them not to spare themselves and to spend their energy to the maximum, which would find its way to the reservoir of energy for the benefit of all.

The third and the most urgent preoccupation for the Elders was watching evolution at work, for the physical bodies of men were becoming redundant, shrinking and becoming smaller and smaller. Only the eyes, nose and ears retained their shape, the earth itself was undergoing upheavals with violent storms, heavy rains and volcanoes roaring and throwing fire to the plains. The Elders understood that both earth and man were getting ready for the next cycle.

CHAPTER XI
THE REPORT - D: AN ODORIFEROUS WORLD

The grinding mill of evolution eroded men's bodies as they became smaller and smaller, long fingers remained to manipulate machines and eyes, ears, noses increased their size. Bellies shrunk and lost the capacity of digestion, nourishment was by pills, sold in government food shops, red pills for breakfast, yellow for lunch and blue for dinner. The pills satisfied the taste buds and contained all the elements necessary to sustain life.' Food machines that produced cooked food were reserved for the elite. Sick people received special pills. As all foodstuffs were produced from chemical combinations of elements from the air, agriculture for food production was at a standstill. The uncultivated land returned to a primeval stage and was covered with forests and wild shrubs.

As man shrunk machines grew more dominant and took over completely, but the dwarfs that men became still retained a strong resentment against the superiority of machines and vent their wrath by occasionally destroying most of them. The Elders of the world government watching the sedition kept silent and let men stew in their own juice for they were inflicting punishment on themselves when they finally calmed down, deprived of sustenance and comfort, men pleaded with the Elders to repair the machines. But if the Elders presumed that they channeled and controlled the aggressive instinct which erupted occasionally, they watched with resignation the process of evolution which, in accordance with the severe and drastic climatic changes reduced men to dwarfs, stumpy little men hopping around the machines they invented and every once in a while destroyed.

One day people woke up to a strong aroma and rushed in frenzy to discover the source. Going around in circles they smelt different odours and after a tedious search they found it was emanating from their own bodies. They rushed and smelled each other to discover that each had emitted a distinct smell. Some were fragrant odours, of jasmine, rose and geranium, others of pine trees or sea wind. They hopped around, in wonder inhaling with their large, inflated noses then they rushed to the street to be enveloped by the smells of the passers-by, some foul and some heavenly. They ran in panic when a stinking smell filled the air, as an acquaintance crossed their path. The veil that covered the inner self was torn; neither thoughts nor feelings could be hidden anymore. Facades with pretensions

221

and false smiles crumbled, the aroma betrayed everyone. Each soul was, naked and smelled! Some, so-called respectable and honourable people, were astonished when they reeked of stinking odours, spreading disgust and repulsion around them. They covered their faces in shame when friends ran away from their path for they were shunned and isolated and hid in their homes until the government started to build retreat clinics for treatment in which they took refuge. People panicked for they did not understand the phenomena and there was no escape from bad smells. Officials tried to assure people by appearing on the screens in town halls to explain that the odours accorded with the Karma and that by exposing the hidden evil thoughts and deeds, atonement becomes possible by shedding envy, hate and greed, it was a process to speed the cycle of Karma. for those who still had many lives to traverse, and was a short cut to purification "as mutation was a short cut to evolution. The cycle of odours they were traversing was an act of mercy of the creator to save people going through myriad lives and to give them a chance to be healed. It was a cleansing stage before purification and signaled that the end of the world was near. The noxious odours that exposed psychopaths, cheats, murderers, rapists and traitors indicated that nobody should despair of God's mercy for treatment was possible for all. Healing was through large doses of energy given by volunteers with fragrant smells and by the "creatures of light," who tended the sick, the infirm, the aged, and willingly bore the onslaught of the stinking odour. Those with the most noxious smells had to do manual labour, a very hard task with their shadowy miniature bodies, but the hardest cases were sent to the north and south poles where they toiled in fishing and building in excessive heat or cold, or to hard tasks in space or under the sea. Atonement was not given, it had to be earned. Progress was monitored and measured through the intensity of smell. Those with the foulest smells had to live in segregated quarters until their Karma was modified as the stink began to fade.

Some stinkers claimed innocence and cried loudly that they had committed neither crime nor evil deed, but were told that evil thoughts had the same power as deeds.

The public at large learned to enjoy the exhibition of deeds and thoughts as they started a guessing game to distinguish the smell of a thief from a cheat or the smell of physical from mental illness, they even discovered that frustration, irritation, affection and love have special smells. They enjoyed the discomfort of lovers who when they said "I love you" to their beloved were repulsed because they emitted a pernicious smell which betrayed inner feelings of which the lover himself was not aware. They walked behind couples guessing at their harmony or disharmony and when the smells differed, parting soon followed but what they enjoyed most was the humiliation of their regional consuls who stood outside the town halls answering questions from the crowd, accompanied by very bad odours which made the crowd boo and hurl insults at the speaker shouting "Liar, your smell betrayed you" and the consul had to be saved from the crowd by the guards and the police. The next day he had no choice but to submit his resignation and disappear in a clinic.

The world became transparent. Not many men who worked in public departments could conserve their posts, nor the religious clerics whose smell exposed their use of their cult, could keep theirs for their own profit. Nobody was safe, except those who had attained purification as the seven Elders. For those who lived in space, under the earth or in the sea, the situation was claustrophobic as it was difficult to escape the bad odours in confined places. Many of them were moved temporarily for a cure on earth while they were being replaced by cases of the hard Karma from earth doing their penance.

Many who felt the shame and humiliation of their own odours became obsessed with the desire for healing so they would smell like a rose. The obsession however worked like a catalyst and hastened the steps to purification.

Human nature in spite of evolution and channeling of basic instincts remained essentially the same, for revisionists and regressionists took the opportunity of the world being busy with the new phenomena to ignore their own stinking smells and to wallow and indulge in grief and lamentation over the death of loved ones. Demonstration of excessive grief over death was prohibited by law and the practice of the death ritual had officially disappeared, it was considered bad taste to even talk about it. The authorities knew about the regressionists but found it difficult to extract grief from their psyche, it lurked in each generation in spite of what they were taught in school that nothing was lost in the universe and that death was not an end but a beginning, but in vain, nothing could appease or comfort them for parting, for loss.

Teachers, intellectuals, writers, told them that the past they lament could be the future, but they persisted and refused to do something about the foul smells of death and grief they carried about with them, the most offensive of all odours . No one could detach and uproot sadness and grief from their souls. And when there was a general outcry and protest from those who were purified, smelling of roses and eager to accede to the next cycle, they were impeded by a foul smelling band clinging to their selfish grief and refusing to modify their Karma. They wondered at the mercy of the Lord who would not abandon a human soul in the dark and who would wait an eternity until each soul by its own free will chooses to undergo the purification

225

which would enable it to enter his realm and his garden of green.

Meanwhile, humanity waited for the revisionists to see reason and rejoiced when they smelled a new perfume, indicating a newcomer into the rank of the purified. Contingents of volunteers were formed to help those with heavily loaded Karmas and slowly and gradually smell of roses and geraniums filled the air while the purified raised their heads to heaven crying "When oh when oh Lord will the whole earth smell like a rose?" Those who complained of the regressive entities who were delaying the rest of humanity relented for the bond of human fellowship grew as they realized that all humanity is one through eternal time and that to condemn one human soul was to condemn all human beings and so their resentment turned to compassion.

Life on earth took on a new aspect during the cycle of perfumes, the earth shook violently, with seas receding and rivers changing their course and mountains springing up in the plains, volcanoes were bursting and forests were growing where it was desert, the climate reversed with the north of the globe hot and dry with monsoon rains and the southern part cooling rapidly with ice and snow. Mutations helped the diminutive humans and animals to adapt. The large heads in the small bodies were shrinking. The birth right machines calculated the amount of energy each individual spent daily, and accordingly indicated food pills to replenish his output. Survival was not difficult as man him-self was pure energy and as such he interacted with his surroundings in a balanced give and take, but once the scale tipped, sickness followed. The purified people who were now the majority were still waiting for the rest to join their ranks. Meanwhile, their desire for food was reduced to the minimum and they began to lose the power of speech, thought translated into smells took the place of words. If one desired to ask another how he was he emitted a smell instead of the question and the answer was a kind of a fragrant perfume. Transformed aromas of human behaviour were modified. A man walking alone on a road may be reliving a painful, past experience or planning a gathering of his clan, passers-by, without giving him a look, could smell his thoughts. The loss of speech was accompanied by the diminishing of the physical body while men became more and more like ethereal shadows who gathered with joy around a newly purified person, inhaling loudly his fragrant perfume and they rejoiced more when the whole earth began to smell of jasmine, frangipani and heliotrope. Soon they thought a universal purification would be achieved as they raised their eyes upwards, ready for the next metamorphosis when they would finally arrive at point omega.

CHAPTER XII

THE REPORT – E: CELESTIAL MUSIC

A fragrant odorous smell enveloped the earth and rose up to heaven, for only the pure now inhabited the world and the first of the purified souls shed their shadowy diminutive physical body and metamorphosed into a note of music, others followed in different scales and different modes, minor and major, high and low, breaking away from the shackles of a hundred thousand year old human species. When the last soul born on the planet earth became a celestial note of music and joined the heavenly spheres, the hand of God was raised and the human orchestra according to the instruments it represented broke into rhythm and harmony in sounds of joy, joy, joy, resounding throughout the universe. The orchestra with its chorus then rearranged itself in high and low, sharp and flat, in its assigned place and sailed between suns and stars beyond count to distant galaxies. On hearing the celestial music the heavenly bodies trembled and hovered in their orbits and danced in pure unadulterated joy. The exquisite sounds in their perfected purity made the sun and moon tingle with pleasure and tinge with adoration. Humanity was paying homage to its cradle, the vast universe with its far recesses, entangled labyrinths, spirals and black holes in a gesture of humility, for it alone had enjoyed the miracle of life, the joy of existence and the feeling of deep sorrow for the inanimate and dead universe enveloped it, so it raised high its melody and the "ecstatic tones of a trillion violins echoed across space and the Lord delighted in his creatures. Far beyond the suns and moons the orchestra sailed to the mysterious invisible dark and heavy area of the heavens which account for eighty per cent of all matter in the universe and on approach to the invisible mass, the musical notes accompanied by the chorus grew louder and sharper until they penetrated the mass of darkness which does not emit or reflect light, but the music caused it to collapse in filaments and clusters in which gas can accumulate and stars can be born.

The orchestra, despite a fruitless search, never lost a dwindling hope of finding the sister planet of their beloved earth which once upon a time according to speculations, held a replica of humanity, a copy of ourselves, but in each case the planet that faintly resembled earth was a sterile, dry and dead world and yet they persisted in the forlorn hope that in an unknown, unmapped corner of the universe they will come joyfully upon life.

No time is recorded for the millions and trillions of years in which the human orchestra toured every corner on its way to the edge of the universe, but its music, which penetrated the darkness, found no edge, the universe has no boundary and no end, it stretches and stretches to nowhere for ever and ever.

Drunk with music and song, the mass of darkness, dark holes and revolving moons kept on dancing and almost broke from their ordained orbits, long after the tunes receded.

The Chaldean high priest who witnessed the scene in a visit to the future in a teleportation machine collapsed at its unearthly beauty and had an epileptic fit, but he described what he saw in delirium and when they succeeded in waking him up from the trance he had had lost his mind, for such scenes are not meant for human eyes and far too far beyond our limited human understanding.

Another Chaldean visionary recorded that the heavenly orchestra traversed the skies like a series of shooting stars. This vision raised the question of time travellers visiting the earth as it recalled an Arabian legend in Syria and Palestine and a similar one in Greece, where a band of Banat al Hur, (daughters of paradise), traversed the heavens with music and song, quick as shooting stars a passage which was taken as an ominous portent of a coming event. Could it be that

230

a time traveller saw the celestial orchestra crossing the skies and told the tale that became a legend?

For how long the orchestra roamed the heavens and its corners without edge, before it came suddenly near to the planet earth which seemed so small, tucked in a corner of a huge, spiral galaxy. The musical notes looked down and beheld their mother earth, their late happy home and a wave of longing seized them, the last vestige of their humanity for in a fraction of time, what it takes between the opening and closing of an eyelid, all the past flashed before them, the chagrin and delight of life lived by man, the miracle of the act of living itself, the beauty of the earth, the light shimmering over a river on a summer afternoon, the blue of the sea and sky, the moon on the water and the gardens of green, the thrill of a voyage, the joy of friendship and the many, many nights of love and natural tears were dropped. The tears filled the dry, scorched and abandoned earth and made it green, the flowers bloomed and rivers flowed, ferns and trees raised their eyes and cooked their ears to drink celestial music and shook violently in homage to those who once peopled the earth, but the notes of joy which soared on first perceiving their lost paradise were transformed into dirges and mourning and farewell for their mother earth, The hummed beat of funeral drums vibrated over their late happy home, the Lord God, the Merciful, the Compassionate on hearing their lament took pity on the frail creatures he created who filled

231

the universe with forlorn music revealing their longing for the past and opened his arms to welcome them unto himself. At the same moment the universe with the planets, the suns, moons and stars collapsed into nothing. From nothing he created the universe and into nothing it reverted and the void prevailed until he wills the Creation of a new universe surpassing in its beauty the old one and in which humanity created by himself and part of himself will take part.

EPILOGUE

It was only when I read the report that I felt vindicated, but not justified, in allowing Abouna to drag me through an incredible adventure. I often wonder whether he lured me and put me in stupor by that musty aroma that prevailed in his quarters or perhaps a drug was slipped into my coffee, or whether it was purely an atavistic reversion to my ancestors. Whatever it was that drove me to accept the proposal, it opened the hidden door of wonderland, a strange and beautiful universe and so when the call came from Stockholm I went immediately.

The Committee of Nine held a meeting with the twenty scholars which I was asked to attend. The subject was about the publication of the prophecy, together with the report, or withholding the publication. The party that insisted on publication said it was immoral to withhold from academic circles and universities a unique document with an untold vision of the universe, besides its value for linguists which may entail a revival of the Aramean language and for historians, philosophers, astronomers and scientists. The prophecy, they argued, would arouse and revive interests in the ancient Aramean; Babylonian and

233

Assyrian civilization and remind the world of their descendants, deprived of their ancient homeland and of their rights.

The opposite party argued that the prophecy is almost impossible to decipher and that the report was only a reconstruction from numbers and symbols with a high percentage of imagination and could be an erroneous interpretation. The effect, of the prophecy on society will be disastrous. They pointed out that the academics were not the only interested party, secret services and military departments put their top agents to find the document in which future wars and machines figure greatly. Rivalry to construct the future machines would be rife. Finally, publication will raise the war cry in many camps.

When the chairman put the question to the vote, only one abstained, which made the vote equally divided. The chairman, a dour young man, suddenly remembered my presence, turned to me and said sarcastically, "according to our agreement with the bishop of Jerusalem, you have the right of veto as the symbolic owner". The statement caused annoyance to some scholars who could not hide the disgust from their faces as if to say that it was ridiculous that the girl from nowhere should decide the fate of the prophecy. I was peeved and said with venom "Gentlemen, I would like to remind you that it was I who found your precious prophecy under a rubbish heap, as to your agreement with the late bishop of Jerusalem, may

Allah have mercy on his soul, the agreement, I believe was entirely to your advantage. As to my decision, knowing full well how anxious many governments are to lay their hands upon it, and not for purely academic reasons, I believe the prophecy should rest on the shelves of the library of Mar Murkus in Jerusalem. It is for a good reason that the future is veiled from us. Let us allow man to find his way blindly to the future, without being warned beforehand".